S.M. LEVINE

Trial Run

First edition

ISBN: 979-8-9919826-1-0

This book was professionally typeset on Reedsy. Find out more at reedsy.com

For Stella

Contents

Preface

Dear Reader,

Thank you so much for choosing my book! Ben and Nell's story is the first in The Well Space series, and these characters are so close to my heart. I love writing imperfect people who find their way to each other, despite not living in a perfect world.

Ben struggles with an anxiety disorder, and he's not very kind to himself about the process. Through the arc of the story, Ben discovers that what he thought of as a weakness might actually be the thing that's made him strong through vulnerability.

Nell has been through a lot, as a single mom working two jobs and looking for a third. This is the reality for so many parents, but she's strong, persistent, a tiny bit secretive and guarded, and above all, a kind person. Learning to open up after past hurts is maybe the hardest journey of all.

Trial Run is an open-door, grumpy-sunshine, age gap contemporary romance. Trigger warnings for the book include: Panic attacks, loss of a sibling (off page), verbal abuse by a partner (off page). If this content might be triggering for you, please take care and consider if reading this book is right for you.

I hope you enjoy these characters as much as I enjoyed writing them.

Happy reading,

S.M. Levine

Introduction

Three weeks to fall in love ... or lose it all.

Dr. Ben Friedman's mental health clinic, The Well Space, has helped hundreds of patients with mental health issues live better lives. But Ben doesn't need any help for himself. He's got it all under control, even though he suffers from worsening panic attacks and hasn't been to the office in a month.

Florist delivery driver Nell uses her green thumb and sheer optimism to get by, but under the surface, her roots are withering. The rent is late, her son is sick, and to top it all off, she woke up to an eviction notice. When she knocks on the wrong door and drops her flower arrangement, it's just one more mistake to smooth over with a smile. But the grumpy, formally dressed man at the door sees right through her cheerful front.

An unexpected connection sparks between them as Nell helps Ben through a panic attack on his porch. To thank her, Ben orders flowers for every patient in his practice. Nell agrees to deliver them—but only if he comes along for the ride. A blossoming attraction in the florist delivery van leads them to try a three-week trial run for dating. Three weeks to see if Ben can step out of his comfort zone, and if Nell can overcome her painful past and nourish her long-forgotten goals.

Chapter 1

The woman on Ben's laptop screen dabbed at her eyes with a tissue, but today's tears were a good sign. For one thing, Penny had her camera on. On bad days, she'd leave it off, and he'd spend the hour speaking to a black square. Ben had rarely seen his patient's face on camera, and it had never looked this relaxed. The usual lines of stress creasing her brow had disappeared, and her eyes were softer.

Penny smoothed a hand over her silver bob and gave him a watery smile.

"I'm ruining my makeup. And I actually put on makeup the last three days. I also got dressed in real clothes this morning. No more pajamas. You can't see, but I'm wearing jeans with a zipper—and a button."

"Impressive." Ben gave her an answering smile, something he only did for patients these days. He was still good at helping clients, but that fact wasn't all that comforting when he was utterly failing at everything else in life right now.

"When you told me three months ago I'd feel like getting

out of bed in the morning again, I didn't believe you. But I think I might be getting past this." She hesitated for a moment before speaking again, her voice revealing a hint of uncertainty. "Don't you?"

"I think you already know the answer. You don't need me to tell you."

Penny squared her shoulders. "I am better. I don't know how else to describe it other than it feels like … like I was under a heavy blanket, and now it's lifted off me."

"That's exactly right. That's what it feels like." Ben swallowed, his eyes ticking to the window of his office before returning to the screen. He cleared his throat and grounded himself in his office chair by connecting to his surroundings. The smooth black leather armrests were familiar under his palms, his home office quiet and lit with a soft yellow light bulb. The crisp cotton of his dress shirt was free of wrinkles, and his tie was neat and straight. In this space, at least, he was in control.

"Depression might always be a part of you," he told her. "But you've learned techniques to help you deal with it, including your new medication. And if it ever gets worse again, you'll know what to do, and where to go for help."

"I will." Penny beamed at him. "And I appreciate you taking the extra time with me today," she went on, dabbing her eyes one last time with her tissue. "I never feel rushed with you. But I hope I'm not making you late."

"Of course not. I build extra time into my schedule for times like this. Let's go over your breathing exercises one more time, then I'll email you the written instructions afterward."

Five minutes later, Ben clicked off the call, pulled off his reading glasses, and pinched the bridge of his nose between his fingers. His life had been reduced to this—a series of video calls.

He shoved his chair away from the desk, stood, and paced the small space. He had to move, before this restless energy swallowed him whole.

On the desktop, sandwiched between two half-geode book-ends, stood his personal copies of each of the three psychology books he'd authored. His framed doctorate degree hung on the wall, alongside his license to practice psychology, clearly visible during his video calls.

To outsiders, he probably appeared to be at the peak of his career. But people weren't what they seemed a lot of the time. People were good at pretending. In fifteen years of practice, he'd learned that much.

The calendar app flashed a reminder at him from his laptop screen, notifying him of his next meeting. He had one hour, then it was back to this new normal, a reality in which he spent his days in this tiny home office because he hadn't been able to drive himself to work for almost a month.

He closed the laptop with a snap and jogged downstairs to the kitchen, where the early spring sunshine streamed in the windows on the front side of the house. On a day like today, most people in the neighborhood would have their windows open.

A flash of white caught his eye as the mailman pulled up to the curb in front of his brick townhome, and his gut clenched. The mail carrier loaded the mail into the cluster of shared mailboxes at the end of the walkway and sped off.

The walk to the mailbox took twenty-six steps there and back, a ridiculous piece of knowledge to have, much less need.

He smoothed a hand down the front of his tailored vest and put a hand to the doorknob. He drew in a slow inhale, using one of the many breathing techniques he'd written about and coached patients through, techniques he shouldn't need to walk to the curb and get the damn mail.

He'd let this get too bad, given in to the anxiety's demands one too many times, and this was where it had gotten him. The longer he went without going out, the worse it felt, everything too bright, too loud. Today might be different, but it probably wouldn't. As soon as he cracked open the door and the warm April morning breezed in, his stomach tightened further.

Leah would laugh her ass off at him if she could see him now, barely able to take a few steps out of his own house. He'd always been the strong one, the one who took care of everything. But she wasn't here to laugh at him now, which was too bad, because it might have snapped him out of this.

He hurried to the mailbox, counting the twenty-six steps, and by the third one, all breathing techniques fled his brain. A woman walking her dog yanked on the chain and the animal yelped. A car rushed around the corner, too fast. Two toddlers chattered and played on a neighbor's lawn.

With a shaking hand, Ben yanked open the mailbox, pulled out the stack of letters, and rushed back inside with a few long strides. He slammed the door shut behind him and sagged against the frame.

It shouldn't be this way, but it was. He'd had it under control before, and it would be again.

He slid the mail onto the counter without looking at it and crossed the room to his treadmill. A quick walk to bring down the tension a notch—not enough to break a sweat in his suit—and then he'd be ready for afternoon appointments. Later, he'd go for a longer run. Five, six, or eight miles to burn away the bad thoughts.

Chapter 1

By next week, he'd go back to the office. He'd push past this last terrible month, because he had to. The clinic and his patients demanded it from him.

He'd set up The Well Space ten years ago in a three-story Victorian house in downtown Kansas City, rather than renting a traditional office space. The quirky building's comfortable furniture and old-fashioned feel helped destigmatize therapy, which many patients resisted at first. The clinic had sky-rocketed in popularity the last few years, as word spread on social media about the velvet couches, kitchen with endless hot chocolate, and family atmosphere.

And they needed him back, stat. That feeling of being needed had always been enough to get him over himself and his own issues in the past, so why wasn't it working now?

He'd just have to suck it up one of these days and go back. Tomorrow, he'd call Cameron. Have his assistant set up some meetings in the office, in person. But he'd do that tomorrow, not today, because he wasn't ready to—

The doorbell chimed, which it never did at this time of day, and he hit the pause button on the treadmill. He wouldn't answer the door, because he never did.

A quick check of the doorbell app on his phone showed a giant bunch of daffodils and a pair of legs. The flowers obscured the face of the person carrying them. He'd never order flowers, his birthday was months away, and anyway, no one ever sent him gifts.

A shattering sound cut through the air, followed by a shriek, and he jumped off the treadmill. He'd jogged to the door and yanked it open before he had time to think.

A woman knelt in a puddle of water on his porch, water soaking the knees of her jeans, surrounded by shards of glass

7

and yellow flowers with wet green stems. Ben froze, his knees locking, because he could not actually slam the door in her face. Leaving her to step on broken glass.

He winced as she reached to pick up one of the larger shards.

"Don't touch that." The words came out harsher than he'd intended, but he was lucky he could form any words at all, because he'd opened this door, and now he had to figure out a way to shut it again.

Her gaze jerked up to him, and Ben lost track of his thoughts.

Her eyes were a light, bright gray, the clear color of a winter sky, startling against the thick dark brown lashes framing them. They were also wide with shock and sheened with tears. She wasn't crying yet, but she wasn't far from it.

"You're not Francine Hays, are you?" Her voice was low and soft, shot through with distress.

"No."

"Any chance you're … Mr. Hayes?" A hint of desperate hope colored the words.

"You've got the wrong address." He managed the clipped answer, then clamped his mouth shut, because his momentary distraction had faded, and now reality came rushing in. A reality in which he was standing at the threshold of his home with the door wide open.

The woman sat back on her heels, her high ponytail of deep brown waves swinging over her shoulder. She took a moment before speaking again.

"Of course it's the wrong house," she said, shaking her head. "I couldn't have gone to the right house, even using my maps app. That would be way too easy for this morning. I'm so sorry I disturbed you."

She shot to her feet, but wobbled on the way up, almost

falling backward into the broken glass.

Ben lunged forward and put a hand on her elbow to help her up. Two things hit him at once. One, she was tall and curvy. She came up almost to his chin, her white sweatshirt soft and thick under his hand. And two, he was fully outside now, close to the dead center of his porch.

He jerked his hand away from her and took a big step backward.

"I'll get the broom. Don't move or you'll step on the glass." That had come out rude at best, but nothing mattered except getting back inside so he could breathe. He hurried back inside to his cleaning supply closet.

It was just the porch. He would not hand off the broom and watch a stranger clean up the mess from the safety of his kitchen. He would go out and sweep up the glass. Quickly, because she was still standing there, framed by the open doorway, waiting for him to return.

He registered more details once he'd made his way back to her. She wore slim jeans, the sweatshirt, and worn blue sneakers. Ordinary clothing, nothing that would make her stand out in a crowd. But her face was unusual. Oval-shaped and pale, with dark winged brows and a strong jaw. A complicated face, not easy to read. And those strange light eyes, glowing gray.

He'd been staring several beats too long. Her chin went up a notch, as if daring him to say something about her mistake.

He cleared his throat and gestured down at the glass shards with the broom handle.

"Stay where you are, and I'll sweep it up."

"If you'll give me the broom, I'm happy to—"

"It's fine," he interrupted. "It'll only take a minute. Don't move."

He took a deep inhale, stepped outside, and began sweeping the area around her feet, starting on her left side and circling around behind her. She stood still, like he'd told her to.

Ben's breath picked up, because it had been a long time—weeks, to be precise—since he'd spent this much time outside, and pretending it wasn't happening didn't seem to be stopping the whole anxiety process.

Pretending to feel fine when you weren't fine was not an advisable coping mechanism. If he were a patient, he'd tell himself not to do it. But he didn't follow much of his own advice these days.

He stood six feet away from the door now. Eight. He swept faster, trying to finish the task before she noticed anything wrong.

"Are you all right?"

Her voice came from far away, down a tunnel of sound. He shook his head, brain buzzing with white noise. He couldn't breathe. All the air in the world had gone somewhere, and that gasping sound in his ears was coming from him.

She removed the broom from his hand gently and leaned it against the wall.

"I think you got all the glass now. Let's go sit down for a minute."

A moment ago, she'd been distressed, but now her entire demeanor changed, her voice softening. She was talking to him like a lost puppy, and it should have been humiliating, but maybe that part would come later, because for now, all he felt was grateful someone else was in charge.

Her cool hand slid into his, and Ben let himself be led to his porch swing, where he hadn't sat in months. He sank down onto the weatherproof cushion, and her soft weight landed beside him. He dropped his head into his hands and tried to catch his breath.

A minute later, the soft pressure of her hand landed on the back of his neck. He startled at the touch, then settled. It had been a long time since anyone had touched him, but he didn't mind the contact in this moment.

"Is that okay?" she asked. When he gave a slight nod, she continued. "My grandma used to get panic attacks. That's what it is, isn't it?"

Ben managed another movement of his head, which he hoped indicated something like "yes."

"Keep your head down. Do you need me to call someone?"

"No. No need." He was more winded than if he'd been running, and all he'd done was stand outside for a few minutes. But it was passing now, the panic leaving his body like a storm moving off on the horizon.

The swing rocked as the woman pushed it back and forth with her foot. The neighborhood sounds faded in intensity, and the world came back into focus.

"What do you normally do when this happens?" she asked after a moment. "What does your doctor tell you to do?"

He huffed a humorless little laugh. "Funny enough, I am a doctor. I should know what to do. But I seem to be having problems going out."

He hadn't meant to say it. The truth he hadn't told any of his family or coworkers, he'd just blurted out to this stranger.

"Oh. Well … What do you do to help it?"

"I wait for it to pass, and it does." Or he avoided certain situations entirely. At least up until now, the strategy had worked.

He kept his eyes on the ground as his vital signs returned to normal. Maybe there was something to be said for waiting out the anxiety, or pushing through it. Or for having someone there to keep you company. And hold your hand like a toddler.

Heat washed into his face, crawling up the back of his neck. The embarrassment he'd been missing a few minutes ago roared to the forefront. He wouldn't be able to look her in the eye again.

He straightened his posture, searching for something resembling his usual control.

"Give me another minute, and I'll be fine." His gaze raked over the spilled flowers. "And I'll pay to replace the flowers."

"Oh no, you don't have to—"

"I insist. I've taken extra time from your morning. And you … helped me out." He cleared his throat, still not looking at her. "Give me the name of the florist and I'll call them with my card."

He scanned his driveway for the florist's van, looking for the name of the business. *Tillie's Flowers* was printed in green on the side of the vehicle, in a scrolling font.

His eyes stopped when they reached the passenger window. Through the glass, a boy's face watched him, brown eyes round with curiosity.

Chapter 2

"Well, I'll get out of your hair."

Nell slapped her hands on her thighs, jumped off the porch swing, and grabbed the broom and dustpan. She quickly swept the pile of glass into it, moving the spilled flowers off to the side one by one, while avoiding the man's cold stare.

The minute he'd seen Marco's head in the window of the van, he'd straightened, eyes narrowing. The last thing she needed was one more person judging her parenting choices, so it was past time to get gone.

She set the full dustpan by the door, picked up the ruined flowers, and straightened, looking anywhere but at the man on the swing.

She tried to stay positive, or at least appear happy on the outside even when things weren't going great, because people were more likely to treat you well when you were pleasant and didn't complain. But this man made it difficult to be cheerful. He'd been rude and cold from the moment he'd opened the door, giving her one-word orders in that harsh tone.

A minute ago, in the middle of his panic attack, he'd seemed vulnerable, in need of help, and she'd reached out to him on instinct. But now he'd pulled himself together again, standing to his impressive full height and smoothing a hand down his vest.

Ever since she'd looked up—and up—at him from her kneeling position, he hadn't smiled once. He'd towered over her with a frown creasing his brow then, and he was doing it again now.

He had black, wavy hair, cut short and brushed back from his face, with liberal threads of silver at the temples. He was older than she was, maybe late thirties or early forties, with sharp features, olive skin, and deep brown eyes.

He wore a three-piece charcoal suit, dressed for court or a funeral, not for hanging out at home in the middle of the morning. His broad-shouldered frame filled out the white dress shirt and vest as if it had been tailored for him. If he had the money to live in this neighborhood, the suit probably had been tailored for him.

To complete the formal look, a white pocket square peeked out of his jacket, silver cufflinks visible at his wrist. Maybe he had a vintage pocket watch hiding in the vest pocket as well.

"Who is that? Your son?" He nodded toward the van window, where Marco's chin still rested on the window frame.

Nell squared her shoulders and forced a smile. "Yes. He's doing fine, I promise. He has snacks and his tablet in there."

Her voice came out a shade defensive, especially since the man kept looking down at her—no, studying her, like a bug on glass. He'd see through her fake smile in another minute, too.

He raised an eyebrow at her, but didn't say anything else,

and somehow that prompted her to go on, to try to explain.

"We had an unusual morning, that's all." Her voice wobbled on the last word, betraying her.

This was shaping up to be the second worst day of her life, and this man's judgemental stare might just be the thing that broke her.

But she didn't have the luxury of breaking down right now. That was for people who had the time and space to curl up in bed and cry. Not for single moms about to be evicted from their rental homes.

She'd woken to a loud banging on her door at 6:37 a.m., which wouldn't have been so early if she'd had any sleep. But sick children didn't care about their parents' sleep schedules, and she'd been up with Marco until close to 3:00.

She'd dragged on an oversized sweatshirt over her sleep shorts and tank, and opened her front door to find Eddy, her landlord, with a packet of papers and a giant cup of coffee in his hand. The coffee wasn't for her, but the eviction papers were.

Even though she'd smiled her most charming smile and explained that her two jobs' paychecks hadn't quite lined up right this week, and she'd have the money for him in another week, he'd shoved the papers into her hand anyway. And told her now she'd have to pay a late fee, along with the rent, or else be evicted.

"You have two days. Then I'm filing them," he'd grunted, and walked off.

Stupid, predatory low-income rental contracts. So many more rules, more penalties, and always, always, less of a safety net. And finding a new place—a landlord who would take her application after she'd been evicted—would be close to impossible.

And the one thing she absolutely would not let herself think about was Marco's adoption agreement. If she couldn't provide a home for him, she wasn't a fit parent.

No one would take her son away from her, though. Because she would find the money in two days. Every other time she'd come close to missing the rent payment, she'd made it work, and this time would be no different. She found a way every time, because she had to find a way.

Marco had reminded her of the reason why by coming downstairs, his face hot, wrapped in a blanket, and completely unfit for school today. For the next forty-eight hours, nothing mattered but scraping together the money.

"An unusual morning," the man on the porch echoed.

He'd probably never had a bill he couldn't pay. His cufflinks would no doubt pay her rent.

Nell forced her biggest, brightest smile. "I guess we all have them sometimes. Anyway. It was nice to meet you …"

"Ben," he supplied, his eyes never leaving her face.

"Ben. I'm Nell. And I'll get out of your way now." A quick escape, and then she could cry in the van. No, later tonight, after Marco was in bed. If he stayed asleep.

"Why is he with you? He's old enough to be in school." Ben's voice was calm, but it held a hint of authority. Like he was used to getting people to tell him things.

And for some reason, she told him. "Of course he goes to school. On normal days. This was the best I could do today."

Ben tilted his head to the side, as if waiting for her to go on, and to her horror, she did go on.

"He had a fever this morning, so I couldn't send him to school. He's got shows to watch and the windows are open. He's fine,

I promise. I'm not a bad mom." Again, that telltale wobble in her voice.

"I didn't say you were." A frown creased his brow.

Another thought occurred to her, even worse than the idea he was judging her parenting.

"Are you really going to call my boss? To try to pay for the flowers?"

"Of course."

"If you do …" She ground the toe of her shoe against his porch in a half circle. "If you do call her, please don't tell her I had him with me today. It's against the rules. I kind of … snuck him into the van this morning."

He gave a sharp nod. "Understood. Nell …" He paused, as if trying out the name. "I'm sorry you've had a rough morning."

With the words, his voice changed, along with his face. She'd thought him cold and aloof. But now his brown eyes softened with compassion, and that was almost worse, because him being nice made her feel everything with twice the intensity.

"It's all right. I guess that makes two of us." She dabbed at her eyes with her sleeve. "Anyway. I hope you feel better. And I'm sorry for interrupting your morning." She turned on her heel to go.

"Is anything else the matter?" He cleared his throat, interrupting her departure. "I don't mean to pry. But you've almost cried twice in the last few minutes."

She rounded on him, still clutching the remnants of the bouquet. "I'm not crying."

"Okay." The word was soft, patient.

And then more words came tumbling out. "But if I were crying, it would be because I'm being evicted in two days if I don't come up with the rent plus a late fee. If I were crying, it would be because my kid was up all night, and neither of us slept, and he is the world's absolute worst napper, so he won't sleep in the car. And I just dropped a seventy-dollar flower arrangement, and even if it's not coming out of my next paycheck—which I doubt—I have to go back to the shop and get a replacement. And explain all of this to my boss, a woman who has apparently never had a bad day. Or a child."

Nell's hand flew up to cover her mouth, as if she could pull the words back inside. Who was this man, and why did she feel like telling him all her problems?

"I'm sorry. I don't usually say those things out loud." She glanced down at her smartwatch and panic threaded through her veins. "And I'm late. I have to go."

Ben stood still on the threshold of his front porch, perma-frown still creasing his forehead.

Nell did what she did best of all, which was erase every trace of tension from her face and smile one last time. It wasn't her most brilliant one, but it would have to do.

"Have a wonderful day, Ben," she said. She shoved the ragged, wet flowers into his hands, turned, and fled down the steps.

She wrenched open the driver's side door, slid into the front seat, and took a couple of steadying breaths, hands at ten and two on the wheel.

"Wh-what was wrong with that man?" Marco's face, with his smooth brown skin and halo of dark curls, appeared between the two bucket seats at the front of the van.

"What do you mean?" she asked, trying to smooth out the edges in her voice.

"Why was he crying? Were you making him feel better?" he asked, his voice scratchy from coughing last night. Her son was far too observant.

18

"He wasn't crying." Thank God she'd dried her own eyes completely before getting into the van. "He was nervous, I think. Or anxious is a better word. I sat with him for a few minutes until he calmed down."

"Y-you dropped the flowers. Maybe he didn't like the mess."

"Maybe so. But I cleaned it up and we'll go back to the shop and get some new ones. Everything will be fine."

"That's okay." He flopped back into his seat. "I'm hot. You need to f-feel my forehead again."

Nell squeezed between the bucket seats of the van into the back, aware she was still parked in front of Ben's house, where he could see her. A hand to Marco's forehead confirmed the fever was back.

"You need more medicine." Keeping her voice light, she fished out the cough medicine and pain reliever from her bag, and gave him tablets of each. He chewed both without complaining, which was even more worrying.

He pulled the blanket she'd brought in the van up against his chin. Nell frowned. Her seven year-old was never cold.

"You should probably keep me home from school tomorrow, too," he rasped.

"We'll see how you are tomorrow." She absolutely could not afford an unpaid day off work at this point. "Do you have enough to drink back there?"

He sighed dramatically. "You packed three juice boxes and two water bottles."

Settling into the nest of blankets and pillows she'd set up for him around his booster seat, he buckled the seatbelt and picked up his tablet again. Flower arrangements surrounded him in the crowded space in the back of the van, making him look like a woodland creature or a cherub.

"Should we listen to more music while we drive?" she asked.

He shook his head. "I'm going to watch another show." He slid on his headphones and sank down lower into the seat.

Nell put the van in reverse and programmed her maps app to go to the next delivery address on her list. Looking at the map now, it was easy to see where she'd mistaken Ben's house for a neighbor's and knocked on the wrong door. Running on no sleep and horrible news was a bad combination. Though she made plenty of mistakes on normal days, too.

She made the next delivery with no issues. Well, other than running over the curb with the edge of her tire while backing out of the woman's driveway. At the bump, Marco looked up from his tablet and rolled his eyes, used to this part of driving with her.

"Sorry!" she called over her shoulder. "Just a bit too far left."

They passed the upscale coffee shop where Nell worked on the weekends, and she swung through the drive through. The perks of working here included four free drinks a week, and today was a day for the frothiest, most sugary coffee drink possible.

After her co-worker handed her the triple shot vanilla latte with extra whipped cream through the little window, some of her sense of well-being returned. With enough caffeine, she could make this work.

She took a long sip and hit the gas.

"Surviving and thriving," she whispered, repeating the catchphrase from the financial well-being podcast she'd been listening to. So the advice on hoarding paychecks and cutting corners hadn't helped much so far. This coffee was free, so it wouldn't deplete her budget.

She glanced back in the rearview mirror, checking on Marco,

who'd checked out watching one of his documentaries. This wasn't how she'd wanted their life to turn out. Struggling to make ends meet. Never slowing down, and never, ever feeling secure enough to think beyond next month.

But you took what life gave you and made the best of it. Even if sometimes, a tiny part of you wished life would give you a freaking break for once. But breaks were rare, and mostly, people let you down, and all you could count on was yourself. Which was great, because she was enough, all on her own.

This evening, she'd start looking at listings for a third part-time job, maybe something online with flexible hours to fit in around everything else.

As for the rent-plus-late-fee, she'd swallow her pride, put on her biggest smile, and ask Amy if she could have her next paycheck early. Her rule-loving boss couldn't find out about Marco tagging along today, though, for the plan to have any chance of working. Maybe she'd pick up a couple extra shifts at the coffee shop, too. Some of her regulars dropped twenties in the tip jar on occasion.

If all else failed, she'd apply for a loan at the sketchy paycheck loan shop downtown, the one with the sky-high interest rates. With her poor credit, a bank would never offer her money.

She turned on her favorite internet radio station, keeping the volume low so it wouldn't interfere with Marco's show, and navigated the afternoon traffic to her next delivery. She'd get the right address. She'd do all the rest of the deliveries seamlessly, make it back to the shop early, and pick up the replacement flowers.

She'd hide Marco in the back of the van, go inside and talk to Amy, and everything would work out fine.

It would be fine, because it had to be. There was no other

option.

* * *

She did not get back early to Tillie's Flowers. Downtown traffic snarls delayed her by over an hour. Sweat stuck to her back as the late afternoon sun poured into the side window of the van.

The shop wasn't much to look at from the outside, just a corner spot in a strip mall. But inside, a riot of flowers and greenery greeted her every morning. Those were the times she loved her job, assembling the day's deliveries of colorful bouquets and potted greenery, inhaling the familiar damp petal smell of the shop.

She threw the van into park and checked the back seat. Marco was asleep, head against the window, his face flushed. Nell put the van into park and dug around in her bag for his medicine. She popped two of the chewable tablets into her palm and climbed into the back seat again.

"Marco." She brushed a hand over his burning forehead. "Little bird. We need to give you more medicine."

"Don't want to." He pushed her hand away and curled up on his side, leaning against the door. He wrapped his skinny arms around his middle.

"Sometimes we all have to do things we don't want to do." Understatement of the year. She scooped a hand behind his neck and pulled him up to a sitting position.

"I d-don't feel good," he groaned.

"I know you don't. This will help." She breathed a sigh of relief when he opened his mouth and chewed the tablets she put in it. "Now drink water, so you stay hydrated."

She was holding the bottle up to his lips when a shadow crossed the window of the van. Nell almost groaned out loud at Amy's bad timing. Her boss frowned at her through the glass, her freckled face red with annoyance and her cropped ginger hair glowing orange in the late afternoon light.

Nell set Marco's head down on the blanket, and he curled up, immediately asleep again in the booster seat. She opened the back door and climbed over his sleeping form, shutting the door softly behind her.

Amy crossed her arms over her chest, pressing her lips together. She stood a head shorter than Nell, so she had to look up.

"I guess you weren't planning to tell me you had him with you today," she said.

"I'm so sorry." Nell smiled as brightly as she could. "But he had a fever, and we got a late start this morning, and—"

"I'm not a fan of excuses. But you already know that. And I don't like making excuses for other people, either. When Mrs. Hayes called and said her delivery never arrived, I told her you were running late, and you'd be there soon. I should have called you. I trusted you'd be there, but maybe I shouldn't have." Her sharp hazel eyes pinned Nell in place.

"I went to the wrong address and I dropped the vase. But I'll pay for it. And I'll take the new flowers to her right now."

"Why didn't you call and let me know what happened?"

"Because I ... I didn't—"

"You didn't want me to know you made a mistake. And you probably didn't want me to find out you had Marco with you."

"Yes." Nell's throat tightened and she dropped her gaze to her sneakers. Amy was about to fire her. It was that kind of day.

Amy cocked her head to the side, considering. "I don't like people hiding things from me."

"I know, and I'm sorry. I'll make it right. I got back as soon as I could, and I'll go out now and deliver the new ones."

"That's what I was going to tell you to do. Until I saw you with your boy." Amy jerked her chin at the back window of the van. "He seems pretty sick."

"He is." Her voice came out almost a whisper.

"Also, if you'd called me, I could have told you about a phone call I got this morning. From a Dr. Ben Friedman. You know him?"

"I … Yes, kind of. He was at the wrong address I went to."

Amy's brow furrowed. "First thing he asked me was, do my drivers take tips, and could he leave one. I said yes, I can process a tip for him. And then he said, he wanted to make sure my driver, Nell, received this tip."

Amy cleared her throat, clearly quoting Ben. "'For her kind assistance on a difficult day,' he said. All formal, just like that. He paid for the flowers you dropped, too."

"Oh." Nell let out a puff of breath. "That was nice of him."

Amy raised an eyebrow at her. "The tip he left you was five hundred dollars."

"He … What?" Nell's mouth dropped open. The tears were back, burning her eyes for the dozenth time today, and she fought them back hard.

Amy studied her face, her expression softening. "Whatever you did to help him out, it obviously meant a lot. Go home, Nell. I'll have Jackie deliver those replacement flowers."

Nell's hand flew to her throat. "You're firing me."

"I'm not firing you," Amy said, sounding exasperated. "I'm

telling you to go home and take care of your boy. And let me know if you need to stay home tomorrow to take care of him. You've got the sick days, you know."

"Okay." Her brain raced ahead. Five hundred dollars plus her coffee shop paycheck would cover the extra late fee on her rent. Why would Ben want to give that much money to her? He had to expect something in return. Gifts like that didn't come without obligations. People always had motives, and sometimes those hidden motives were a nasty surprise.

But she was too damn poor to refuse the money, and Amy had just given her a free pass to go home. She'd take the opportunity to escape, and think about the rest later. Relief flooded her system, and with it, a wave of exhaustion.

On impulse, she reached out and squeezed Amy's upper arm. "Thank you."

"Don't thank me. Thank him."

Chapter 3

Ben studied his daffodils as he ate his usual breakfast—a protein bar and black coffee—standing at his kitchen counter. He'd put the flowers in a pitcher two days ago, and they hadn't started to wilt yet. Tillie's sold high-quality flowers, he'd give them that.

Every time he walked into the kitchen, the yellow cup-shaped blooms reminded him of the woman who'd barged her way into his brain with a shattering of glass.

Nell's expression had been so bright as she'd handed him the flowers. If he hadn't heard her bleak description of her morning a few minutes before, he'd almost have believed her smile was real.

The huge tip had probably been a mistake. She might not want a stranger offering her money. But he couldn't do nothing, not after what she'd told him about being evicted and her son being sick.

She'd seen him at his worst, and hadn't judged him. She was, in fact, the only person who knew the state of him right now.

Her eyes appeared in his mind throughout the day, distracting him from work.

The obvious way to ease his conscience and get her out of his head was to help her out. Then he wouldn't feel this nagging sense of worry that she wasn't okay. He'd never see her again, anyway.

In a few short minutes, she'd changed his situation, though. He'd sat with her on his porch and told her the ridiculous truth.

I seem to be having problems, he'd said. And saying it aloud made it that much more real.

His laptop chirped with a video call a few minutes after he'd settled at his desk upstairs, and Vanessa's face appeared on the screen when he clicked the answer button.

"Ben, it's been forever." Her voice was cheerful and upbeat, but her brows lowered with worry. As the co-founder of the clinic and his long-time friend, she'd seen all his moods, and her current level of concern was not comforting. She leaned in closer to her screen, as if she could examine him through it, her auburn waves filling the entire screen. Her cat-eye reading glasses made her green eyes look comically large.

"It has been awhile." Ben tried to project confidence in his tone, keeping his arms relaxed on the armrests of the desk chair.

"And how are things going there? Work's not too fast-paced?" Now she was using her therapist's voice on him, never a good sign. It was the kind of question you'd ask a pleasant stranger, and Vanessa had known him forever.

"Good. I've had a couple of new clients come on board this month."

"Good. That's good. And … working from home is still your preference right now?"

"Quit beating around the bush and ask what you really want to ask," he snapped. If she wanted to pry, she should go ahead and try it, rather than treating him like one of her patients.

"Fine." She flopped back in her pink velvet wingback chair and gave a dramatic sigh. "Damn it, Ben. I wish you'd talk to me about what's going on."

At least she sounded more like herself now.

Ben cleared his throat and prepared his usual excuses. Oh, but they were getting harder to spit out.

"I've told you. I have a few extra things on my plate right now, and working from home is more flexible. But I'd like to come in one day soon to make sure everything's in order at the clinic. I'll schedule a time with Cameron."

"Only one day, though?" She cocked her head to the side.

"I'll start with one and see how it goes." Most likely, it wouldn't go. At all.

Vanessa drew in a breath, started to say something else, then closed her mouth. A minute later, she tried again.

"Ben. How you run your practice is your business. And I don't want to pry into your private life. Even though we've been friends for … How long was it?" She tapped her chin with a finger, pretending to think. "Ten years?"

"So don't. Don't pry. Trust that I know what I'm doing." He had no idea what he was doing.

"Okay." She drew in a breath, focusing on the camera. "And what about the conference in Chicago next month? Are you still planning on going to accept the award?"

The Well Space had been nominated for a national award, recognizing their innovations in therapy and the patient experience. But getting on a plane to attend the conference would be about as easy as getting to the moon.

28

"I don't have the plane tickets yet, but I'll get them booked soon." He swallowed. "But it wouldn't be a bad idea to have a backup person, in case—"

"A backup person?" Her voice rose sharply. "That's not a good idea, and you know it. People come to those conferences to see you. If we win the award, you have to be the one to accept it."

"I know I'm the one who wrote the books—"

"You put The Well Space on the map."

"But you and I came up with the concept for the space together. We started it as partners. It's your place as much as mine, and you know it."

"It is, but I'm not the one people want to see. You've always been the face of the clinic. If you can't go, we'll need to cancel the clinic's attendance altogether." Vanessa made a slashing gesture across the camera.

"We won't need to cancel it." Ben ground his molars together. "It's still two months away."

"And we haven't seen you in weeks." Vanessa's eyes flashed, her rare temper making an appearance. "I want to respect your privacy, but this isn't just about you anymore. It's affecting everything."

"What do you mean?" He sat up straighter in his chair.

She cleared her throat. "We've seen some ups and downs with patient intake levels over the years."

"We have."

"Well. I thought you'd want to know we're losing people. We're at our lowest number of patients in two years. People are leaving for the new startup on the north side of town. Harmonious Mind."

"The one that's imitating us?" Ben lunged out of the chair

and paced the room. Vanessa would just have to deal with seeing his legs pass back and forth across her screen.

"The very one." She rubbed a hand over her forehead. "Look. People talk. They haven't seen you around the clinic. Someone started a rumor you're leaving the practice."

"That's not true and you know it."

"Do I?" She raised a brow. "You're not telling me much these days."

"I'm not leaving the practice. I'd tell you if I was considering it, and you know I'd never keep something like that from you."

Ben shoved a hand through his hair and stopped pacing long enough to meet her eyes. "You know what I put into starting the clinic. You know what it means to me. I'd never just—"

"Disappear?" she supplied. "But it kind of looks that way, doesn't it?"

"I'm not disappearing. I'm still here. I promise." A note of desperation crept into his voice.

She leaned closer, her eyes softening. "I'm sorry, Ben. I'm really sorry if there's something going on with you I don't understand. But I can't understand it if you won't tell me anything."

"It's personal." Ben's gaze slid away from the camera.

"So you've said, and I hope you can find a way through it. We need you around here. No one dresses up as fine as you do. You keep the place pretty."

He snorted a laugh. "Nice try."

Her expression turned earnest. "Please take care of yourself. And let me know if I can help."

"I don't need any help." It was a colossal lie. "And I'll come back soon. You have my word."

"All right." She sounded somewhat convinced.

"And will you tell people, if they ask, that you've spoken to me, and I am definitely not leaving?"

Vanessa frowned. "I'll try. I'm not sure they'll believe me, though. They want to see your face, Ben."

"They want to see my face." He transferred the call to his phone and paced downstairs, not caring that it was un-professional, and Vanessa could see his living room in the background.

"There's nothing special about my face. There's nothing—"

He stopped short when he reached his kitchen, where the flowers were a bright spot of color amid the steel appliances and granite countertops.

"Vanessa."

"What?"

"People like getting flowers, don't they?"

"Who doesn't like flowers? Why are you asking?"

"Nothing. I just … had an idea for a minute there."

"Keep having those good ideas, champ," she said, her tone fond. "That's what got us where we are now."

"Will do." He regarded the flowers, his mind whirring with possibilities.

"You know …" Vanessa leaned toward the camera. "You look a little bit like the old Ben right now."

"What do you mean?"

"I can't put my finger on it. But your eyes lit up a minute ago. When you asked about the flowers."

"You're imagining things."

"I'll have you know, I'm very observant." She straightened her glasses frames.

"Well, go observe a patient. I've got a few calls to make."

"Bye, Ben."

She clicked off the call with a wave, but Ben was already setting his phone on the counter.

Everyone liked flowers, and flowers would be a great way to reconnect with his patients. If he ordered flowers for every patient in the practice, that would show them he cared, and he wasn't going anywhere.

He couldn't lose his practice, not because of this … particular weakness of his. And flowers could be a first step to going back, an apology for his absence. He'd call Cameron and have his assistant send him the full client list with all the addresses. His patients had already opted in to receive mail and deliveries from the clinic. He'd send these flowers, using his own money.

If Nell worked on commission, even better. A large order might give her another financial boost. He could say she'd sold him the flowers.

And after sending the flowers to his patients, he'd go back to the office. As soon as possible.

The four walls of his townhome suddenly felt more confining than they had for the last four weeks. If he could just go for a run outside like he used to, his sneakers eating up the long miles, then everything would make sense again. At the memory, his body perked up like a dog hearing the word "walk." He needed to get out, to *move*.

He made it as far as the front door, hesitated with his hand on the knob, and thunked his head against the wooden panel.

He would try again tomorrow.

He picked up the phone and called Tillie's Flowers.

* * *

Chapter 3

The next morning, Ben startled when the doorbell rang. It couldn't be who his imagination told him it might be, and yet a glance at the doorbell camera showed Nell's face.

He ran a nervous hand over his vest front as he strode to answer the door. His heart thudded underneath the vest, rushing in his ears. If he didn't go outside, he should be fine to stand in the doorway and have a normal conversation.

"Hello." Her expression was guarded, but she looked better rested today. She must have gotten some sleep. She held a tall potted plant in her hands, the wide, waxy green leaves obscuring most of her torso.

"Good morning." He cleared his throat. "I'm assuming this time, it's not a mistaken delivery?"

"No, this is for you." She held the plant out to him and he took it automatically. "To say thank you. For the tip."

She didn't sound very happy about it.

"It was nothing," he said, studying the plant in his hands so he wouldn't look past her and see the porch and the front yard.

"It wasn't nothing." She pinned him with a direct look. "It was more money than anyone's ever given me. Why did you do it?"

"Because—" He drew in a sharp breath, chest tightening.

Her expression changed, softening. "I'm sorry. It's hard for you to stand out here. I forgot. Would you … Can I come inside?"

"Of course." He took a big step backward, relief loosening his throat as soon as the door shut behind her.

She stood still for a moment, her eyes wide as she took in his kitchen, which was state-of-the-art, but also pretty bare, truth be told.

Her eyes landed on the daffodils. "You kept them."

33

"I didn't want to waste them." Ben set the potted plant on his countertop, next to the flowers. "And how is your son?"

Her gaze swung around to him. "Better. He's hardly ever sick, but when he does catch something, he gets over it fast. I'm lucky."

"Good. That's good." Now that she stood inside his house, looking up at him with eyes as luminous and complex as he'd remembered, his train of thought eluded him.

"So. The tip." She crossed her arms over her chest and leaned a hip on his counter. She wore a white T-shirt and black joggers today, her hair in the same high ponytail.

"You want to know why I left it for you."

"I do. And I also want to know why last night, my boss called and told me you placed an order for 174 flower arrangements. You told her I sold those flowers to you, but I didn't."

"She told me for larger orders, like weddings, her employees earn a commission. So I gave her your name."

"But I didn't sell you anything," she repeated.

Ben folded his arms over his chest, mirroring her posture. "You did, in a way, the other day. You convinced me that flowers are good for people's mental health. So I sent flowers to my therapy patients."

"You're a therapist. I thought you said you were a doctor."

"I am. I have a doctorate in psychology. I can even prescribe medications for my patients."

Nell processed that for a moment. "And the flowers are ... to cheer up your patients?"

"Yes."

"But why me? Don't answer that." She pressed a hand to her forehead, looking embarrassed. "I know you felt sorry for me the other day. I said too much about my situation. But I'm

34

fine."

"You said your landlord—"

"Really, we're doing okay. I'm looking for another job, and I know something will work out for me. I wish I hadn't said all that."

She dropped her hand and met his eyes again, dead serious. "Nobody gives someone a five hundred dollar tip and a commission worth another two thousand if they don't want something in return."

"What? No—"

"What do you want from me? Because I don't date, if that's what you were hoping for. I won't." Her chin went up a notch.

Outrage climbed up his throat. "That is *not* what I meant. I'd never ask for that in exchange for a gift." He filed her statement away for later, though, because the therapist in him needed to know why she didn't date.

"Then why?"

Ben searched for the right words. "I wanted to help you. Partly because you needed it. But also because you helped me."

And I couldn't get your face out of my mind.

Nell stared at him, her expression shifting from disbelief to confusion. "I didn't help you very much. I sat with you for five minutes."

"It helped." Best to keep the explanation simple. No need to tell her that no one else in his life knew how bad he'd gotten. "And this was something I could do in return. Something that would benefit both of us. My patients get flowers, and you get a commission."

"Yeah, but it's too much. I can't take it. I can't be indebted to you like this."

"You need the money, though."

She dropped her head, her ponytail swishing forward to cover half her face. "Yeah. I need the money."

"It's okay to accept a gift."

"No." Her head snapped up again. "Not from a stranger. Not that much money. But I'll pay you back. I can work on your lawn on the weekends. I'm good with landscaping."

"You don't need to do that." His townhome had a team of landscapers who kept every lawn looking almost too perfect.

"Please let me do something." Her eyes begged him to understand, and Ben couldn't say no. Her pride wouldn't let her accept the money otherwise.

"Well. You did help me with … No. That's a bad idea."

"What? What were you about to say?"

"When you sat with me on the porch, I got over my … problem a lot faster than usual. And I had the thought I could go with you one time when you deliver the flowers. As a way to test the waters. Get out of the house."

As soon as the words were out, he wanted to take them back. Of all the stupid ideas.

"You want to deliver flowers with me," she said.

"I told you, it's probably a bad—"

"It's a great idea." Her eyes lit with purpose. "I can help you get out of the house as a way to pay you back. That many flowers will take three or four days to deliver at least. Maybe a week."

Ben held up a hand. "Can we start with one day? Maybe even one errand."

One hour might be too much for him, in all honesty. But the earnest hope in her face was too much for him to squash this terrible idea now.

"Okay. One day. We're ordering the flowers now, but a big

order takes a few days to come in. They should be in the shop by Monday. I could pick you up at 8:30?"

"8:30 on Monday," he repeated, heart pounding in his chest. What had he just agreed to?

"Great! I'll see you then." She stepped away from the counter and smiled up at him, her first genuine smile since walking in the door. "And thank you. I really do mean it. That money … It was the nicest thing anyone's ever done for me."

She was breaking his heart. "I told you, it wasn't that much—"

"But it was." She gave a nod and turned to go. She'd reached the door when Ben stopped her with a question.

"What kind of plant is that? The one you brought today."

"Oh. It's a ficus. Some people call it a rubber tree. It reminded me of you, I guess. Because it's tough. And it grows without much sunlight."

"I—" Ben was rarely at a loss for words. "Thank you."

She gave him a small smile over her shoulder and shut the door behind her.

He crossed the space to the counter and adjusted the ficus so it stood closer to the daffodils. He stood there for a long time, looking at both plants. Nell was pure sunshine, and he was … what he was.

She'd already seen him at his worst, so it couldn't hurt to try going out with her on one small errand. She was the only person who'd witnessed his panic attacks, and while it wouldn't be ideal for her to see another one, at least it wouldn't be a surprise.

It could be good practice, for when he went back to the office. He'd call his doctor today and ask about changing the dosage of his anxiety med, to be safe. This could be the first step to getting his life back together, pulling his own weight again. Some plants needed less sunlight, and maybe that was okay.

Chapter 4

A swarm of dragonflies swirled in Nell's stomach as she pulled up the florist van in front of Ben's house. And it was natural to be nervous, because an intimidating, scowly man who'd given her two thousand dollars on a whim would be delivering flowers with her today. Maybe all week.

She'd had to sit down when Amy had told her about Ben's huge flower order, and the amount of her commission.

Amy had been overjoyed at the large sale for the shop. She'd actually smiled at Nell and thanked her for making the sale. Then her face had taken on a knowing look.

"Sounds like this Dr. Ben has a thing for you," she'd said.

Nell had denied it to her boss, but of course, no one gave a gift that big for no reason. So she'd gone to his house to clear it up. She'd gone there intending to tell Ben he had it all wrong if he expected a date in return for his money. She'd half expected to throw the money in his face and be back at square one with this month's financial crisis.

But she did need that money. It would save her ass this

month, and probably next month, too.

So instead of cutting things off with Ben, she'd gotten herself further involved in … whatever this was. When he'd half-suggested he could come with her on her deliveries, she'd jumped on the chance. It was a way to pay him back, to not be in his debt. Her company was one thing she could offer in exchange for the huge favor he'd done her.

And he did need help. She'd seen it for herself. Some plants needed a bit more attention to grow, and the same was true of people. And she could never resist a dying plant.

Mom had always said when you were having a hard time, helping someone else out was one of the best ways to feel better. Nell couldn't change her own situation, but maybe she could do something small to change Ben's.

She could drive him around on a few errands this week, accept his money without any guilt, and maybe help him with his panic attacks in the process. A win-win exchange. He'd take her help and go on with his life, like everyone did, leaving her to figure out how she'd survive next month.

She'd stopped by her landlord's office this morning and given him her entire coffee shop paycheck, plus Ben's tip from the other day. She'd start worrying about next month's rent later.

But today, the sun was shining, she had a van full of rioting blooms and greenery, and no bills hanging over her head. Today was a good day, and even if Ben scowled at her the whole time, she would be helpful and cheerful. That was how she would pay him back.

Still, her stomach swooped again when he opened the door. He wore a navy suit today, but he hadn't put on the jacket yet. His crisp white shirt was rolled up to the elbows, revealing the roped muscles of his forearms.

Chapter 4

Doctors weren't supposed to have muscles like that, and they weren't supposed to smell nice, like bay leaves and cedar. In an office, or another setting, she might have felt intimidated by the perfection of his appearance.

He was just a person, though. A person who might be very nervous about today.

She turned her gaze upward and gave him a big smile. "Good morning."

"Good morning." Ben stood frozen in the doorway, his posture stiff.

She'd started to understand that what seemed like formality in his manners was at least partly anxiety. His spine was too rigid, his hand gripping the doorknob as if it was the only thing holding him up.

"Are you ready to go?" she asked, keeping her tone light and easy.

"Almost. I need my shoes." He turned on his heel and went back inside, without inviting her in. Nell followed, shutting the door behind her.

A man who was always as dressed-up as Ben wouldn't forget to put on his shoes, or his jacket. Was he stalling for time? The thought softened her further.

Now fully inside his house, she scanned the room. She'd known he lived in a lot nicer part of town than she did, but the difference between their homes was stark. His kitchen was moodboard-perfect, with gleaming stainless appliances and granite countertops. The ficus and the daffodils still stood on the counter, the only splash of color in the place.

She peered into the living room. The open space was decorated in a minimalist style, with beige and white furniture and simple modern artwork with geometric designs on the walls. No family photos here, but maybe those were in another room.

Ben sat on the couch tying his shoes, and watching him swiftly deal with the laces felt oddly personal. He stood and shrugged on his suit jacket, then crossed over to a side table and slid his keys and wallet into the pockets of the suit.

Here in his own space, he was confident and put together, moving easily with no sign of anxiety. This must be what he was like in his normal life, in his work. A man in charge of his surroundings. A man people would look at and admire.

She shifted her eyes away so she could stop admiring him. Because he wasn't just what he looked like. He was dealing with his own problems, like everyone else did.

"Oh. You have a rock collection," she said, her gaze landing on the colorful display on the wall. Rows of shelves by the fireplace displayed crystals and rocks, most unidentifiable from across the room. A rose quartz, maybe, and something purple.

"They're not gemstones. None of them has much value, other than sentimental." He turned toward her, patting down his pockets as if to make sure he hadn't forgotten anything.

"Where did you get them?"

"Some of them I found outside. Others I bought at rock and mineral shows. I used to collect them—" He shook his head, cutting himself off. "I think I'm ready to go. Or as ready as I will be."

Nell tamped down her curiosity and pulled her phone out of her pocket.

"I've got the delivery list ready to go. It looks like Beverly Jackson is about to get a pot of hydrangeas."

"Beverly?" His brow creased. "I had no idea she lived near

me."

"She lives a couple blocks away. And she's going to love these flowers. We'll try the one errand, and see how it goes, like you said the other day."

Nell made her voice as bright and encouraging as possible, because Ben's expression right now looked a lot like Marco's before he vomited.

Ben was silent for a long minute. "I think riding in the car won't be so bad for me. The hard part will be getting from the door to the van. I'm not good with the … With open spaces." He winced, as if the admission cost him.

"If it doesn't work out, I'll walk you right back inside. I won't leave you alone, I promise."

Ben met her gaze, seeming to steady himself. "All right. Let's go."

They walked to the front door, and beside her, Ben tensed up.

She paused with her hand on the doorknob. "Just walking to the van."

Ben drew in a breath. "Just to the van. I can't believe I agreed to this."

"Will it help if we walk fast?" she asked.

"I think so. Let's try that."

Nell nodded, opened the door, and stepped outside. Ben followed her onto the porch, locking the door behind him. His chest rose and fell, already faster than it had been a minute ago.

On instinct, Nell looped her arm through his, linking them together at the crook of his elbow. He startled, then curled his arm up, keeping their arms locked. He shook his head, as if he regretted needing the help.

"Together?" She smiled up at him.

He gave a tight nod, and took his first steps away from the house. They hurried across the porch, then took the four steps down to the front yard.

"You've got this. A few more feet down the sidewalk, and we're in the van." His arm shook where it threaded through hers, but he propelled himself forward. His legs were a lot longer than hers, and she hurried to keep up.

"Almost there." She clicked the key fob to unlock the van and opened the passenger door for him. He launched himself into the seat and slammed the door shut.

Nell jogged around to the driver's side and opened her own door. She slid into the seat and looked across at him.

Ben rested a shaking hand on his brow. Maybe she'd pushed too far, and it had been too much. Maybe he was having a panic attack right now.

"We can go back inside. If you need to, that's fine. I'll walk you right back," she offered.

He didn't say anything.

"Ben? I need to know if you're okay. Was that too much? I'm sorry if it was. We can always try it again some other time."

After what felt like an hour, he lifted his head. A tiny smile curled the corner of his mouth.

"I did it," he said, his voice shocked.

Nell couldn't help the huge grin that took over her face. "You did."

"I'm not going back inside." He lifted his chin. "That was the hardest part, and the rest will be easier." He said it with authority, as if trying to convince himself the words were true.

"Okay." She started the ignition, the smile still stuck on her face. "Driving won't bother you? You're really okay in here?"

"I think I am." He shook his head in disbelief. "I don't quite believe it."

"Then let's go to Beverly's house." She put the van in drive and pulled away from the curb.

Ben took up a lot of space in the van, and sitting this close to him, she could feel the tension in his body, and the warmth. His aftershave scent mingled with the damp greenery and flowers in the van.

"How did you end up delivering flowers? Did you always want to be a florist?" he asked.

She gave a quick glance in his direction. Other than his death grip on the door frame, he was looking straight ahead out the windshield. He probably needed conversation to distract him from the fact they were picking up speed, turning onto a larger street.

She gave a little laugh. "Nope. This wasn't the original plan. But life threw me a few curveballs and here I am."

"What did you want to do before? If you don't mind my asking."

"I was in a degree program for horticulture at the university. I was the first person in my family to go to college. My mom was so proud. She died of cancer when I was in my third year."

"I'm sorry."

"It's okay. It was a long time ago."

She felt Ben's gaze on the side of her face. As usual, he had a way of listening that made her want to talk more. He didn't judge. He understood all the ways life got complicated.

She took a deep breath and went on. "Anyway, my plan in college was to start a landscape design business. But I dropped out to get married a few months after Mom died. That changed everything for me, made me question everything. I only had a

45

year left before graduation, too. At the time, I thought I could finish school later, but ..."

"Other things happened?" he supplied.

"Right. I ended up on my own with a kid. A single mom, like my mom was. I never thought I'd be like her, but history repeated itself there."

"That must have been hard."

Ben didn't ask where Marco's dad was, like so many people did. He just listened, and him being a good listener was very dangerous, because there were a lot of things about her marriage she'd never told anyone, and she didn't intend to start now.

After this week, she'd never see him again, and she wasn't about to expose all her inner hurts to another person guaranteed to disappear from her life.

"It was hard," she said lightly. "But I'm doing fine."

She kept her hands at ten and two on the wheel as she navigated the rest of the way to their stop.

* * *

Ben's patient was thrilled with her new flower arrangement. When the older Black woman answered the door, her first expression had been confusion, which transformed into delight when she saw the sender's name on the card.

"Oh, this is so beautiful." Beverly turned the flower pot one way and then the other, admiring the deep indigo blooms from different angles. "And they're from Dr. Friedman. How thoughtful of him."

"Yes, I'm out delivering a big order from him today."

"I'm not surprised he did this. He's an amazing doctor. I'll definitely send him a thank you note, because these made my day."

"Flowers will do that, won't they?" Nell gave the woman a warm smile.

"You're absolutely right."

Beverly squinted over Nell's shoulder, across her driveway at the parked van.

"Is that Dr. Friedman in the car with you?" she asked, her voice filled with confusion. "It's hard to see with the reflection on the windows. But I thought I saw someone who looks like him in the front seat."

Nell froze, unsure if Ben would want his patients to know he was here with her. She hadn't asked him about this part.

She gave a nervous laugh. "Just a friend of mine who came along with me. The glare is really bright out this time of day."

"Of course." Beverly gave another long look at the van, as if trying to see past the glare. "Well. Thank you again, my dear."

"Have a wonderful day."

Nell jogged down the steps and climbed back into the van. Ben was staring out the windshield with a strange expression on his face.

"She loved the flowers," Nell told him.

"I'm glad." His jaw ticked. "She saw me, didn't she?"

"She couldn't see very much past the glare on the windows. But she asked if it was you. She thought she recognized you."

"What did you tell her?"

"That I had a friend with me. I didn't tell her who it was. I wasn't sure if you—"

"This was a mistake." Ben cut her off. "Why didn't I think

about the fact people were going to see me? That they'd know—
"

"Know what? You wanted to send them flowers? That's considered a nice thing to do, you know."

He shook his head hard. "It's unusual behavior for me. Think about it. What would a doctor be doing in a florist's van?"

His sharp tone brought Nell's head up. Right. His job was a lot more important than hers.

She drew her spine up straight. "I'll take you home, then."

"That would be best." He set his jaw. "And I shouldn't come with you again tomorrow. Once was enough."

"But it helped you. You left the house, and you haven't for a while, right?"

She couldn't resist prodding him a little. He'd made progress today, and that was worth something.

"It did help. But I shouldn't do it again. People might see me."

"And that's such a bad thing."

"With how I am now? Yes, it is," he snapped. He'd gone rigid in the seat next to her, hands in fists on his thighs.

"All right. We'll head back then." Nell backed the van out and made the turn onto the main road again. There was no point in arguing. She was here to help him, here to be cheerful, not to question him. That was their deal.

She could have helped him more, if he'd let her. But as usual, she wasn't going to get what she wanted.

He was silent for a few minutes before speaking again. "She looked so happy. I haven't seen her in person in a while." He cleared his throat. "You must enjoy this part of your job. Making other people happy."

She nodded. "That's the best part. A lot of times, the flowers are a complete surprise to people. The looks on their faces when they get them ... It's a lot of fun. Other parts, like downtown traffic, are not so fun. And getting lost. And dropping vases."

She tried to make a joke out of their first meeting, but he didn't laugh.

"That could have happened to anyone," he said.

"Yeah, well. Those kinds of things seem to happen to me a lot. Which is why I am where I am in life."

"I don't understand."

He sounded genuinely confused, when it should have been obvious to anyone she was a disaster and a half.

Exasperated, Nell whipped around to face him at the stop light. "I'm careless. I drop things, I'm late all the time, and I can't organize my bills right. I bend all the rules at work. I'm not supposed to have you in the van with me, either."

"I didn't know that."

"Well, now you know. I'm ninety percent chaos. That's why I'm twenty-eight now, and working for a florist is where I'm at. Which is fine for someone like me." She tried to keep her voice casual, but her throat closed on the last word.

"What do you mean, someone like you?" His voice sharpened.

"Someone who doesn't have a lot of skills." She said it lightly, but the words burned her throat. Someone who didn't have a lot of options in life was closer to the truth.

"Why would you think that?" His gaze stayed on her as she drove the few blocks back to his house, winding through the residential area.

"It's nothing. It's just ... It's something I've learned about myself. Lots of people have told me. I'm kind of a mess. I never

49

seem to be able to get ahead of things."

She pulled the van up to the curb and threw it into park with more force than she'd meant to.

Kurt had told her all those things about herself, told her every day, and the words still lived inside her, coiled in the pit of her stomach. Her ex had told her not to finish college, that she wouldn't need a job. She should rely on him to take care of the finances, because she'd never be able to keep track of it all.

He'd been right about some of it, though. Here she was, scrambling to make rent again. A more organized person wouldn't have this issue. A better mom would have—

"Nell. Look at me." Ben's voice was low, commanding. She swallowed and turned slowly to meet his eyes, which were softer than she'd ever seen them, an endless deep brown well of understanding. No wonder his patients loved him so much.

"Please don't say things like that about yourself," he said. "I don't know who made you believe those things, but they're not true. You have many skills, and you can learn anything you want to. You got me out the door of my house, and no one's done that in a month. I'm forty, and that's where I'm at."

Nell froze, her hands stuck in their place on the steering wheel. Something in her chest cracked open, letting out a swirl of nameless emotion. She pushed the feeling away, but it kept expanding, a giant pressure behind her ribcage.

She gave a hiccupy little laugh. "Okay. I guess I have one skill."

"One skill among many." Ben's gaze was steady on her. "You know a lot about plants. You take very good care of your son. Above all, you're a kind person who cares about other people, and that is a strength of its own. I hope you hear that. And I may need your assistance to get back inside my house, if you don't mind."

"I don't mind." Nell jumped out of the van to avoid his eyes. One more minute of their kind compassion, and she'd lose it.

The dozen steps back to his front door went by fast, much easier than the trip out to the van. He kept her arm looped in his the whole time.

All the way up to his porch, her heart beat a wild tempo, the fissure in her chest expanding. She swallowed down the emotion and made her face as neutral as she could. She couldn't even manage a fake smile right now.

Once Ben had unlocked the door, he turned to face her, safely back inside his house. "You have more flowers to deliver tomorrow, I assume."

"Yeah." She looked over his shoulder, anywhere but at his face.

"Well. Good luck. And thank you for today. I'm glad to know I can manage going out for a short time, at least." He gave her a nod of dismissal and shut the door with a click.

Nell walked back to the van at a normal pace. In the driver's seat, she opened her delivery list and tried to make a plan of where to go next, but her thoughts were a tangle of thorns and vines. She opened her maps app, chest heaving, but the map swam in front of her eyes.

She dropped her forehead onto the steering wheel and burst into tears. The happy mask she wore most of the time fell away, and feelings rushed out, water from a broken vase. Someone had seen her, for the first time in so long. And it was a relief, and a terrible pain at the same time.

She wiped her eyes with a sleeve and pulled the van away from the curb before he looked out the window and noticed her still sitting out here. At least no one had witnessed this meltdown. She could keep this to herself, keep it together.

She didn't drop anything, or go to any wrong addresses all day.

Chapter 5

Ben had just finished his evening run on the treadmill when his phone chimed with a call, in Vanessa's ringtone. Hopping off the machine, he mopped his brow with the hem of his T-shirt and swiped to answer the call.

"It's after six. Why are you still in the office?"

"Hello to you, too. And there've been a hundred times I could've asked you the same thing." The "until recently" was implied in her tone.

"You should go home. Get some dinner." Ben strode into the kitchen, filled a glass of water, and drained it in a couple of gulps.

"I will soon. I was catching up on some patient paperwork. But I had to call you and say, nice work on the flowers. We got several phone calls about them today."

Ben set down the glass. "Did they like them?"

"Of course they liked them. Everyone likes flowers. It was a good idea you had."

"Thanks."

"No substitute for seeing you in person, of course." And now she'd gotten to the real reason for her call.

"Of course." Ben kept his tone casual. "That's why I called Cameron and had him set up some in-office appointments for me."

"Really?" Vanessa's voice rose with excitement. "That's great news, Ben."

"Yes, really." He swallowed. "By next Monday, I'll be back, at least part time."

He'd instructed Cameron to book him for one or two appointments in the mornings, not the full day. He might not be ready for that yet.

"This is wonderful news. And … you're sure everything's okay?" A hint of uncertainty crept into her tone.

"Everything's fine, like I told you. I'm ready to get back to the office." He was absolutely not ready.

"Well. It'll be great to have you back."

"I'll see you next week."

Ben clicked off the call and paced back into his living room. He stood halfway between the kitchen and the stairs, studying the shelves holding his rock collection. All the walks he'd gone on with Leah, looking for sparkly stones. All the times he'd stopped mid-run to pick up a piece of quartz she'd like. His little sister had always had a weakness for things that glittered, and he'd always taken care of his sister.

The one-year anniversary of her death was only a few weeks away now, and he owed it to her memory to pull himself together.

So he'd taken the step of calling Cameron, officially committing himself to going back to work in person. He'd also booked his plane tickets to Chicago, clicking the purchase button before he had time to back out. He would go on that trip. Even though he'd only left his home once in the last month.

Today's van ride with Nell had been the first step. If he could go out once, he could do it again. Doubtless, increasing his anxiety medication had helped him avoid a panic attack today, but so had Nell's steady, cheerful presence.

Still, he'd been right to call off any future outings with her. The danger of one of his patients spotting him was too great. He'd never survive the embarrassment if they figured out why he'd been absent, why he'd needed to send the flowers in the first place.

But the look on Nell's face as they'd parted ate at him. She'd looked … shattered. He rubbed the center of his chest, where an ache had formed under his breastbone. She'd shared some of her past with him, with hints of painful memories.

Everything in him had wanted to ask her more, to have another chance to talk to her. And not because he wanted to help her as a therapist. He could see her becoming a friend, and friends listened to each other's problems.

But he couldn't involve her any more in his own issues. She didn't need to see any more of his anxiety, and she definitely wasn't responsible for hiding him from his patients. She wasn't even supposed to have him in the van with her. It was better this way, with him handling his problems on his own.

If only he had proof he could leave the house by himself. Tomorrow, he'd make himself try it alone, even if it killed him.

But he didn't get the chance to try it alone, because the next morning, at 8:30 sharp, Nell rang his doorbell.

He went to the door and pulled it open as if he'd been

expecting her, which was ridiculous, because he hadn't been. Still, his heart jumped under his tie at the sight of her, in her leggings, T-shirt, and ponytail, face free of makeup and looking up at him cautiously, as if she wasn't sure of her welcome.

"Good morning." His voice came out rough around the edges, and he cleared his throat.

"Good morning. I'm here to take you out again." Her voice lifted on the last word, edging it into a question.

"I don't ... I told you yesterday—"

"Not for a delivery," she rushed on. "It's for a ... pick-up? I have an errand to do before I start the flower deliveries today, and I thought you might want to come. For the practice. If that would work for you?"

"A pick-up?"

"It's just some plants I need to relocate. But you wouldn't have to see any of your patients, and you'd get out of the house again." Her expression was open, pleading with him to agree, as if she really wanted him to come along.

"Why did you come back?"

Her gaze shifted to the side. "Because I promised I'd help you. In exchange for the commission."

Of course. She still felt indebted to him. It had nothing to do with the strange, one-sided feeling of connection he'd developed yesterday, talking with her.

"I suppose I could come on an errand."

Relief brightened her expression. "That's great. Whenever you're ready."

Like yesterday, Ben allowed himself to be led to the van by one arm. Nell's arm was bare below the elbow, and he could feel the heat of her skin through the cotton weave of his dress shirt. He was barely winded when they got into the vehicle.

"Better today," she observed.

"I think so."

"So it's good I came back." The words came out tentative, as if she was unsure she'd done the right thing. And he knew that about her now, that she wasn't sure of herself, of her own strengths.

"Yes. It's a good thing you came back."

The smile she beamed at him made his chest hurt.

"This drive will be a bit longer," she said. "About fifteen minutes to the hardware store, and then I'll drop you back at home."

"The flower shop buys plants from the hardware store?"

"They're not for the shop. They're … You'll see."

They drove in silence for a couple of minutes before she spoke again, seeming uncertain how to start.

"Yesterday, what you said to me …"

"I want to apologize. I pried too much into your personal life, and maybe I shouldn't have."

Nell shook her head. "I'm not sorry you asked about it. What you said … It meant a lot. And that's part of why I had to come back again today. How did you know the right thing to say?"

Ben shifted around on the seat. She'd been honest with him, and he could do the same.

"I could say it's because it's my job. That I do therapy sessions all day. But the truth is, we have a few things in common."

Nell glanced at him in surprise, silently encouraging him to go on.

"You lost your mom, and I lost my little sister a year ago. Leah."

Her mouth turned down. "I'm so sorry."

"Well. You were talking about losing your mom, and how it

set you adrift, or made you question a lot of things in your life. And I think … I've probably been going through something similar."

"Tell me about her. If you want to. Sometimes it helps."

Ben gazed steadily out the passenger window. He'd tell her this, and hope speaking the words wasn't too much for him right now, out here on this bright street.

"Leah was born with a genetic condition. Prader-Willi syndrome. She had intellectual disabilities as well as physical ones, and she lived in a residential facility as an adult, where they helped her out. I used to visit her all the time, and we'd go on walks at least three times a week. She was … light. Happy all the time. She had a way of making me pull my head out of my ass and be in the moment."

"It sounds like you had a great relationship."

"We were close. I helped take care of her a lot when we were growing up. She was only thirty-two when she died. She caught a respiratory virus most people would have fought off, but her body was weaker to start with."

He cleared his throat, which had tightened up. "Anyway. I guess I'm saying I understand your loss. And I wasn't just playing therapist with you yesterday."

"Thank you for telling me." She reached out, as if she wanted to put her hand on top of his where it rested on the seat, but then she thought better of it and pulled away.

Strange, but he felt the ghost of what that contact might have felt like. He'd held her hand the first day they'd met.

She cleared her throat. "I thought a lot about what you said about me the other day."

"If it was too much—"

"No, it was perfect. But it was a lot. You made me realize

how much I've let … certain people in my life tell me things about myself. Things that maybe weren't all true."

"This is about your marriage." He didn't know why he was so sure of the fact.

She gave a sharp nod. "Yes. But I don't want to talk about my ex."

"But that's why you don't date."

"That's why. I can't take a chance of a bad relationship again. I won't do that to Marco."

Or herself. She'd been hurt by someone, badly enough that she'd pushed everyone away. Ben's hand balled into a fist on his thigh, but he kept his tone light as he answered.

"I don't date much, either."

Her brows rose in surprise. "Why not? I'd think a good-looking doctor would—" She snapped her mouth shut, as if realizing what she'd admitted. Nell thought he was good-looking.

"I guess I've always been different in that department. I have to get to know a woman before I feel any attraction at all. And I've been told I'm hard to get to know."

A smile lifted the corner of her mouth. "You are kind of reserved."

"That's the word. Are we here?"

Nell had pulled the van into the large parking lot of a chain hardware store. She drove up to the curb, where rows of shriveled-up potted plants stood in neat rows.

"Yep. This is our pickup."

"Nell. These plants are dead."

She shot him a grin. "That's what everyone thinks. But they're not really."

"So you pick up dead plants and … do what with them?"

"I take them home and fix them up. It's fun. And the stores just give them away when they're like this."

"So this isn't for the flower shop."

"Oh, no. It's a hobby."

"And you're probably not supposed to have these in the florist van, either." He couldn't prevent a smile.

"Nope." The sheer impish joy on her face lit up something inside his chest, kindling a spark of warmth there. "Wanna help me load them in the van? You can stand in the back and I'll hand them up to you."

"All right."

Ben folded his long frame between the front bucket seats, slid past the short bench seat in the back, and waited. When Nell opened the rear double doors, bright sunlight flooded the open space at the back of the van. The sides of the vehicle were lined with shelves, where the bouquets to be delivered stood in buckets of water, with vases and pots contained behind the guard rails.

Nell hoisted up two plastic pots from the curb. "Just set them on the floor there."

He took the thin, black plastic pots full of dried-out soil and spindly brown stems and lined them up in careful rows.

They worked for a few minutes in silence, Nell handing him two pots at a time. She'd take home at least a dozen dead plants today. And they did look dead.

They'd fallen into a rhythm working together, when several things assaulted his senses at once.

Nell was sweating lightly, a sheen of it on her forehead and dampening her pale blue T-shirt. The shadowy valley between her breasts was visible in the V-neck of the shirt from his vantage point above her. When she twisted her torso to retrieve more pots from the curb, the shirt rode higher in the back, highlighting the curve of her rear end.

Her hips were generous and soft, tapered in at the waist, and her neck was long and pale, which was right where he'd put his lips to taste the hollow of her throat—

He inhaled sharply, because no, that would not be happening. Of all the inappropriate times to develop a sudden awareness of her body. She'd told him more than once she didn't date, and he would respect those boundaries.

"All done," she said, brushing her hands off on her now very dusty leggings. She gave him a beaming smile, and another wash of heat went through him. "And you've been standing right by the van door for five minutes. That's amazing."

"I guess I have." He hadn't noticed the time pass. Apparently being slapped in the face by lust was a good distraction.

"I can take you back home now."

"Yes. I have appointments this morning."

Once they were buckled back in, Nell turned to him. "Come out with me again tomorrow. I'll be delivering your flowers the rest of the week. You can hide out in the back seat of the van, and none of your patients will see you there. It's just, I think this is helping you. Don't you?"

She wanted to help him more than he wanted it himself. And he already knew he had a problem with saying no to her.

"I think you're right. I'll come with you again tomorrow. And I'll ride in the back, like you said."

The back seat would be better. Farther away from her. Ben kept his eyes on the road the whole way home. Because something long-dead had roared to life inside him, and oh God, tomorrow was going to be torture.

Chapter 6

By the end of the week, Ben had made important progress. He'd walked to the van unassisted. He'd gone out for more than one errand, riding along as Nell delivered flowers to several of his patients in a row. Last night, he'd gone outside by himself, after sundown, and walked himself to his car.

He'd sat inside the black luxury sedan by himself, not starting the ignition, but with both hands on the wheel. Practice for when he'd do it by himself next week.

He hadn't made any progress in banishing his sudden, inconvenient attraction to Nell, however. And today was the last day of their delivery runs. She'd told him yesterday that Marco would be with her today, because his school had an inservice day. It was a good thing they wouldn't be alone together. A very good thing, because otherwise he might do something stupid like ask her out.

She didn't want that from him. And she shouldn't. He was a dozen years older than her, and she'd been through a lot. It

Chapter 6

wouldn't be right to ask for something she didn't want to give, the very thing she'd told him from the start she would not do. Especially because he'd given her money.

Still, he caught himself staring a lot. At her striking eyes, the color of slate under a running river, gray and bright at the same time. He'd be in the middle of a sentence and forget what he'd meant to say, but luckily she hadn't seemed to notice him trailing off. She stopped his brain.

He noticed everything about her now. Once he'd started, it was hard to stop. He noticed the sweep of her thick ponytail across her shoulders. Her long, elegant fingers. And she had the most amazing curves that he absolutely should not be watching at all as she ran up the steps to deliver flowers.

She'd never know his thoughts, and that was a good thing. He had a lot of practice hiding those, pretending to be calm on the outside when the inside of him was a brew of tension. Or in this case, a pure sensual fog.

In the close space of the van, her citrusy shampoo filled his nose, cutting through the scent of the flowers. His fingers itched to touch the velvet-smooth skin of her jaw.

This was very bad. He'd been so isolated, he'd latched onto the first person who'd been kind to him in months. That had to be the explanation. Except now he'd been out of the house five days in a row, he hadn't seen anyone else remotely interesting.

He'd told her he was rarely attracted to anyone, which was true, and which had probably made her feel safe from any advances from him. He'd be the biggest hypocrite to turn around and ask to see her again after today.

No, today would be their final outing, and then they'd both return to their normal lives. Their time together was up, and after this, they wouldn't see one another again.

So it was a good thing she would have Marco with her again in the delivery van today. Overall, a very good thing. On impulse, Ben grabbed both halves of a small geode off his display shelf and pocketed them before heading to the front door.

"I hope you don't mind sharing the back seat with another passenger today," Nell greeted him when he opened the door.

"Not at all." His eyes ate her up, taking in every detail before he forced himself to look away. "How many stops do we have this morning?"

"Want to try for five?"

"Five it is."

"He probably won't talk to you. Marco." She walked alongside him down the steps, matching his long strides. "He doesn't talk to strangers very much. But if he does warm up to you, you'll hear lots of facts about life on the ocean floor or fossils."

"Ah, a future scientist."

"Maybe so." She smiled her sunshine smile at him, the genuine one, which he could now easily distinguish from the fake one. Her mouth was full and wide, her eyes crinkled at the corners.

He didn't need to hold her arm as they walked anymore, which was good, because he also didn't need the reminder of how she fit next to him, right at shoulder height. At this point, he wouldn't be able to walk and feel her against him at the same time.

He slid into the back seat and found himself face to face with Nell's second-grader, who sat in a booster seat printed with dinosaurs. Marco wore Hawaiian print board shorts and a red T-shirt, and he held a tablet in his lap, but ignored it in favor of staring at Ben. His expression wasn't hostile, but it wasn't friendly, either.

Ben swallowed his embarrassment at riding in the back seat like a child. Alone, it hadn't felt so bad, but sitting next to Marco brought home the fact that he hadn't been brave enough to face the front seat since the first day.

"Good morning," Ben said.

Big brown eyes continued to stare at him, but Marco didn't say a word. His black curls stuck out in every direction, overlong. Nell probably had a hard time making herself cut her son's riotous hair, because she liked to make things grow.

"Marco, this is Ben," Nell said. "I told you he's been helping me do deliveries this week."

"I heard you have the day off of school," he told Marco.

Marco gave a tiny nod and put his headphones back on. He pressed play on the tablet and ignored both of them.

Nell glanced over her shoulder as she pulled the van away from the curb. "He doesn't mean to be rude. He's just shy."

"I understand. It's not a problem."

"He was a tiny bit jealous of you. He asked me why he couldn't come with me every day. He's not the biggest fan of school."

"Any particular reason?"

"He doesn't talk a lot about it. But I know the kids teased him last year, about how he talks. He had speech delays when he was younger. He's doing much better now with help from the speech therapist. He trips up on some words, but it only comes out when he's stressed now."

"The right therapy can make a big difference."

"And how are you feeling today?" she asked.

"What do you mean?" Ben twisted to look at her. She

couldn't have guessed all the inappropriate thoughts he'd been having. Usually he was harder to read.

"I just meant you've done a lot of new things this week," she said. "And this is our last day."

"I feel better. This week has been good for me."

"I think so too. So do you think it was worth it? The money, I mean?"

"This was never about you paying me back. Not for me." Ben's voice came out sharper than he'd meant it to.

"Oh, I know it wasn't—"

"But it was for you, wasn't it? You hated taking the money."

She swallowed. "Well, it was a lot of money. And you had no reason to give it."

"Like I told you at the beginning, I wanted to thank you. You helped me, and I wanted to do something in return."

"Then I guess we helped each other. I'm glad." Her soft voice reached out to him, and he wanted to wrap himself up in it, to hear it every day.

"Me too." Ben swallowed, his throat tight. That sounded like a goodbye. He turned to face the window and watched the outside world pass by.

The world wasn't such a bad place, from inside the van. With company, and the flowers crowding them close. With the knowledge he was doing something good for his patients, and with a person he'd come to think of as a friend by his side.

The world was harsh and bright, but sometimes, with the people who mattered nearby, the ride could be … surprisingly enjoyable.

A few minutes later, they arrived at the first stop. Nell retrieved a bouquet from the back, carnations and tulips, all in shades of pink. She ran up the steps to knock on the door of the next recipient.

When Ben turned to check on Marco, he discovered the boy's eyes already fixed on him. They studied him as if Ben was a strange animal.

"I heard you like to learn about the ocean and fossils," Ben told him.

Silence was the reply, but he still had Marco's attention.

"I like science, too. I collect rocks, or I used to, anyway." He pulled the geode out of his pocket, keeping the two halves pressed together. "I used to go running outside a lot on the nature trails near my house, and I'd find all sorts of fossils and gems. I also found a lot of geodes. Have you ever seen one?"

Marco shook his head. His eyes flicked down to Ben's hand, where he held the oval brown rock.

"It's a kind of rock with crystals hidden inside. From the outside, it looks ordinary. I picked this one out of the dirt near the trail. I took it to a rock shop and asked them to cut it in half with a special saw. And look."

He broke the two halves of the rock apart, revealing the dark purple crystals lining the interior. Marco's jaw fell open.

"These crystals are called amethyst. But you never know what you'll find inside a geode. They can be all different colors—white, green, or pink, too. The surprise is part of the fun."

Ben held out the rock. "Do you want to look at it?"

Little fingers brushed his as Marco took the rock from his hand. He turned the pieces around, twisting the two halves until he figured out how to put them back together into a seamless whole.

Ben smiled and turned to face forward, just as Nell returned from her delivery.

"Everything going okay in here?" she asked.

"Fine," Ben said.

As they drove to the next delivery stop, Marco played with the geode halves, opening and closing them. After a few minutes, he clutched the halves in his fist. He hadn't gone back to watching the show on his tablet.

The next time Nell got out of the van, Ben turned to face Marco again.

"I bet you'd like looking for geodes the next time you're outside. Do you want to know the secret of how to find them?"

Marco nodded, his expression serious.

"I'll tell you my best rock-hunting tips. First, you look for a rock that's rounded, like an egg or a golf ball. A lot of geodes have a hollowed out interior, and it affects the shape of the rock on the outside."

Marco nodded again.

"Two, you look for rocks with a bumpy exterior. Like the peel of an orange. And three, you can tap it, to see if it sounds hollow. It might feel lighter than a normal rock, too, because there's air inside."

Ben kept up the one-sided conversation as they did the rest of the deliveries. Marco never replied, but he listened the whole time. As they made the last stop, he turned again to face the boy.

"You can keep it, if you want to."

Marco's eyes widened.

"Th-thank you." His voice was quiet and rough, an old man's voice in a seven year-old's body. As soon as he'd spoken, he pressed his lips together tightly.

"You're welcome. Maybe you'll find some crystals for your mom. Do you think she'd like them?"

"Sh-she would. She likes colors."

"Good." He turned once more to face the front of the van, ignoring the rush of satisfaction that filled him.

It shouldn't matter that he'd earned a few words from Nell's quiet son. He would never find out whether Marco went rock hunting or not. A tightening sensation in his chest accompanied the thought.

A few minutes later, Nell dropped back into her seat and started the van.

"We'd better take you back home. If you want, I can text you when we finish the last of the deliveries to your patients. So you know it's all done."

"I'd like that."

She pulled out her phone and opened her contacts, and Ben told her his number.

Nell was quiet as they drove back. Marco returned to watching TV on his tablet, headphones over his ears.

The air in the van was thick with flowers and leaves, and her citrus-scented hair, and he'd miss all of this, even though it had only been a week. He would miss her.

When they pulled up at his house, she killed the ignition and turned to him.

"Well. I hope things keep getting better for you." She fiddled with the keychain, flipping it between her fingers. Was it his imagination, or did she seem to be stalling?

"And you as well."

"They will. I'm looking for a third job. To make ends meet better."

He frowned. "I didn't know you had a second job."

Nell rolled her eyes at him. "Of course I have a second job. It's still not quite enough, though. Your money was nice, but it can't solve all my problems."

She said it playfully, but Ben's chest tightened further. He hadn't improved her life at all. He'd temporarily helped the problem, but now she was right back where she'd been last month.

She'd improved his life in a lasting, real way. And he'd given her money, something far less valuable.

She fiddled with the keychain some more, and Ben didn't make a move to get out of the van yet.

"Do you want me to walk you to the door?" she asked, after another minute of the awkward silence.

"No. I can manage it myself. Thanks to you."

"You have to stop thanking me. I did nothing."

"It wasn't nothing to me," he said fiercely. "I'm only sorry I can't—" He shut his mouth, shook his head to clear it. "You deserve more. You deserve for someone to see all the good things about you, and appreciate them. So I will say thank you. And … Goodbye, I guess."

"Goodbye, Ben." Her voice held a hint of a wobble, but he wouldn't analyze that right now. The week was over, and it was time to walk himself back into his house, back into his real life. Next week, he'd pick up right where he'd left off at the clinic.

He took the dozen steps to his door in long strides, covering the ground in seconds. He kept his head down, not looking at the sky or the neighbors' yards, or the cars parked on the street. With single-minded focus, he made it to the door, unlocked it, and let himself inside. He wasn't even winded.

This was how he'd do it next week. Fast, no distractions. No giving in to his anxiety, and definitely no enjoying the scenery.

He turned and gave Nell a single wave, and she waved back,

put the van into drive, and pulled away from the curb. Marco's eyes watched him from the rear window as they pulled away.

Ben shut the door to his house. It was quiet and cool inside. He toed off his shoes onto the wood floor, and the soft click echoed in the entryway. He walked into the living room and looked around, as if he was a stranger seeing the pale, lifeless room for the first time.

He'd been fine alone here for a month, but nothing felt the same now. He sank down onto the plush white couch, letting the silence of the house swallow him up.

Chapter 7

Marco talked about Ben and his geode all afternoon as they finished the floral deliveries, and most of the way back to the flower shop. His non-stop chatter filled the van, making her smile.

Did she know what a geode was? Ben was an expert at finding geodes, and he'd told Marco all the ways to spot them. Could they take rocks they found outside to the rock shop to get them sawed in half? Maybe they could cut them in half at home with the toolkit.

Marco hadn't been so animated in a long time. He held up the rock Ben had given him, demonstrating how the two halves fit together for her to admire in the rearview mirror.

"From the outside, it j-just looks like an ordinary rock," he told her.

"It absolutely does."

"And you never know what's going to be inside. It could be any color, not just purple, like this one. Or there might be nothing inside."

"It must be so exciting to cut them open." Nell smiled over her shoulder at him.

"We have to try it. Can we look for rocks tomorrow at the park?"

"I have work tomorrow, but maybe Sunday." Tomorrow she had her weekly shift at the coffee shop.

"Okay. And when we find one, we have to show it to Ben. I know we'll find at least one."

"Well … I can't promise that."

"Why not?" Marco demanded, his voice turning stubborn.

"Today was the last time he planned to come with me. He was only helping deliver the flowers he'd sent to the patients at his clinic. But now we're all done. Ben is very busy, and so are we, so we might not see him again."

"But you said he needed help. You said he was shy, and he needed practice with going outside of his house."

"I did say that." His memory was too good. She'd always told him as much of the truth as she could. And he always remembered, and brought it up at the worst times.

He crossed his arms over his chest. "W-why can't we keep helping him? He looked sad when he left."

"I don't think he wants any more help right now. He has a lot to think about."

But Ben had looked sad when he'd said goodbye. She wouldn't examine too closely the answering emotion that had swelled inside her, watching him walk up his sidewalk alone, because it was pointless to feel anything more for him. They'd connected, helped each other out, and now their time together was over. She'd paid him back for the enormous favor he'd done her, and that was that.

Marco huffed out a loud sigh and looked out the window.

"If we find a geode, we have to show it to him," he repeated.

"We'll see. Maybe."

Marco went silent for the last stretch of the drive, showing her he was mad at her by putting his headphones back on and twisting his whole body in the booster seat to face the side door. He looked about as uncomfortable as she felt. Uncomfortable and off balance.

Something had changed inside her since the first delivery day with Ben. The landscape had shifted and she'd seen her life from a different angle, like an optical illusion concealing an image right in front of her. Now there was no unseeing it.

She'd been putting one foot in front of the other for so long after Kurt left, just trying to survive. But she'd wanted other things before. The eighteen year-old version of herself had been so sure of her path.

Her sketchbooks full of fantastical garden designs lived in boxes in her storage closet, but they also still lived inside her brain. They were still real, even though college was out of reach for her now. The money alone, not to mention the course schedule, made it an impossible dream.

But the fact she was even thinking about it—that was new. Those old desires had been buried deep. And then Ben had come along and cracked her open like an acorn, and now the memories wouldn't go back to sleep.

That had to be why it had been so difficult to say goodbye to him. For all his formal, reserved exterior, he'd seen inside her, to the secrets she kept hidden even from herself.

And he'd looked sad to leave. Sad and aloof, untouchable as the first day they'd met. But she had touched him. She'd threaded her arm through his, felt the warm muscle under the fine wool of his jacket. Under the formalwear, he was just a man. A man she didn't need anything else from, because she'd never need a man again.

But that didn't mean she couldn't start making some changes now.

Back at Tillie's, she slammed the van door shut with too much force, causing Marco to pull off his headphones and stare at her. She jogged around to his side of the van and opened the door.

"Come on, we're going inside," she told him.

His forehead scrunched up. "But I usually wait out here."

"Not today."

She'd finished all the deliveries, and she needed to ask Amy about her commission payment. And if Amy found out she'd had Marco along with her in the van again today, so be it. She hadn't been fired last time.

Let Amy know how hard she had to work to balance everything. This was her real life, and she wouldn't hide it any more, like it was something to be ashamed of.

She waved at Jackie, who was working the front counter today, grabbed Marco's hand, and slid behind the front desk into the back hallway. The smell of flowers and damp greenery filled the air. She tapped on the door of Amy's office, where her boss sat at her desk, working on her computer. Marco stood behind her, half hidden in the doorway.

Nell stuck her head in the door. "Just dropping the van keys off. We're all done with the deliveries."

"Great news. Come on in." Amy swiveled around in her office chair just as Nell opened the door all the way, revealing Marco. Amy's eyes flicked between her and her son, and her brows raised, but she didn't say anything.

"He didn't have school today. Inservice." Nell squared her

shoulders, ready for whatever criticism Amy wanted to throw her way.

"It's fine," Amy said, her tone clipped with what could be irritation, or maybe it was just her usual short manners.

Nell cleared her throat. "Anyway. I wanted to ask you about my commission. If I could possibly have the money today, that would be great."

"Of course. I'll get you a check." Amy pulled open the top desk drawer and took out the checkbook.

Her hand hesitated over the book, pen in mid-air. "Thank you for bringing in this sale, by the way. It was a big boost for us this quarter."

"I didn't do much. I did him a favor, and I guess this was his way of paying me back."

"Well, this is a nice payment." Amy handed her the check, and her heart did a little flip at the number on it.

Her boss paused for a moment before speaking again.

"Nell. When he called me that first day, he said you helped him on a difficult day. Did he mean it was a difficult day for him, or for you?"

Nell gave a nervous little laugh. "I think we'd both had a difficult day. I got an eviction notice that morning, and Marco got sick. I wasn't at my best. I'm sorry for breaking your rules, though."

Amy frowned and shoved a hand through her short hair. "No, I've been thinking a lot since that day. And maybe the rules need to change. I didn't think before about how things must be for you, as a single mom, and I should have. So I want you to know, you can bring Marco along with you, anytime you need to."

"Really? That's amazing. Thank you so much. You have no

idea how much." Nell's hand squeezed Marco's, probably a bit too tightly, and he plastered his torso to her leg, something he only did when he was feeling uncertain.

Amy gave a short nod. "I want this job to work for you. You're a good employee, and I'm trying to be … more flexible. My wife says I'm too much of a hardass." Her mouth twisted up in a half smile.

"Oh, well I …" Nell paused, unwilling to confirm Amy's wife's opinion, but she sent the woman silent thanks. "This will help me out so much. Thank you, again. "

"Good." Amy gave a sharp nod and went back to her desk, clearly uncomfortable with the emotion in the room. "Good. Have a good weekend, then. And you too, Marco." She started typing again, dismissing them.

Nell backed out of the doorway and shut the door. She dropped the keys to the delivery van on their usual hook by the front desk and patted her pocket, feeling for the check. The bell on the door jingled on the way out.

"She wasn't mad." Marco said, as they crossed the parking lot to her car.

"She really wasn't." Nell put a hand on his shoulder. "Lucky us."

* * *

That night, after boxed macaroni and cheese—the only kind Marco would eat—they watched a documentary together. Marco had forgotten he was mad at her. Or more likely, he was saving up his arguments until later, to be used at bedtime.

No doubt he'd chosen this show about rock formations on purpose.

They sat on the couch together, a bowl of trail mix between them, with Marco's body folded in half, knees at his chest. One by one, he picked out all the chocolate chips from the bowl and ate them.

"It's a good thing I love you so much, or I'd be mad you left me with all the raisins," she told him.

"But you like raisins, and I don't." He sifted through the bowl, finding more pieces of chocolate.

"I like chocolate, too."

"I'll share the chocolate with you if you put more in the bowl. I promise." He gave her a devious grin, then turned his gaze back to the screen. "You're missing the volcano eruption. The lava is made of melted rock."

"It's pretty amazing."

"If you put a stick in the lava, it'd catch on fire in two seconds."

"I bet you're right."

"Too bad there's no volcanoes in Missouri." He sighed and ate another handful of chocolate.

"I always thought that was a positive thing." She handed him a paper towel, hoping to avoid melted chocolate from his hands making it onto the couch upholstery.

After the show, she got him into the bath. His weekly hair wash day added forty minutes to their bedtime routine, but she loved finger-coiling his curls one by one so they dried in perfect ringlets. Since adopting her biracial son, whose birth mom was Puerto Rican and his dad white, she'd tested dozens of curl products until she found the ones his hair liked.

After he was tucked into bed, she turned on his star projector night light, and he tucked his stuffed brontosaurus under his left arm.

"Tomorrow I'm going to Carla's house, right?" he asked. Their neighbor watched him on the weekend days Nell worked at the coffee shop, in exchange for Nell helping clean her house a few hours a week.

"That's right. I'm making everyone in the city their coffee tomorrow morning." She reached out and smoothed the hair away from his forehead. How much longer would he let her do that? "But Sunday is our day together this weekend."

"And we'll go to the park and look for rocks." His brown eyes reflected the dim light of the night light as they searched her face.

"Yes. We can go Sunday."

"We're going to find a geode," he said, a hundred percent sure of the fact.

They probably wouldn't find a geode. He'd have to be disappointed by life sooner or later, but holding off that disappointment as long as possible for him was part of her job as a mom.

"I hope you're right. And goodnight."

"Goodnight. We'll find one. You'll see." He turned over on his side and pulled the covers up to his chin.

Nell slipped out of the room, leaving his door cracked open. Downstairs, she folded two loads of laundry, loaded the dishwasher, and swept the cracked linoleum of her kitchen floor. Her landlord should replace the floor soon, but he wouldn't.

She moved on to her evening plant care routine. She added one ice cube to each orchid pot, so the plants would receive a slow drip of water, then removed dead leaves from her philodendrons and misted them with water. The expensive bird's nest fern she'd brought home from the flower shop was still drooping, though. Jackie had over-watered the sensitive plant until it almost died. Nell had brought it home like a stray cat, but she'd return it to the shop when it recovered.

"Come on, Oscar," she told the plant. "Let's try you by the other window and see if that's better." She carried the fern from the dining room to the living room and set it on the windowsill. Lifting the edges of the plant, she checked the bottom of the pot, where she'd added some gravel to help the soil drain.

Exhaustion from the long day caught up with her and she sank onto the couch. She dug through her purse for the check from Amy and deposited it into her bank account using her bank app. Then she wrote out a check for next month's rent and tucked it into her wallet. She'd give it to Eddy tomorrow morning.

She'd never been ahead on rent payments. Not once in six years. For now, at least, she and Marco were safe. Thanks to Ben.

She'd put off texting him ever since they'd gotten home, but she'd said she would let him know when they'd finished the deliveries. She pulled up his name in her contacts, opened a message thread, and typed a text. She typed and then deleted a smiley face emoji. He was probably one of those people who used perfect grammar and punctuation in all his texts.

Her thumb hovered over the send button. Was 10:00 p.m. too late to text? Before she could analyze it any more, she hit send.

Deliveries all finished this afternoon.

Right away, three dots appeared on the screen. They flashed and disappeared several times. After a minute, she received a short reply.

Glad to hear it.

> *Thank you for the geode you gave Marco. He loves it.*

He's very welcome.

She watched the open message thread until the phone screen went black, then set the device on the couch cushion next to her.

That rock probably meant nothing to Ben. He'd brought it along on a whim to show her son. It didn't mean anything, and she shouldn't feel any way about it at all—

Her phone buzzed with another text.

Do you want to see my clinic? I'd like to show it to you. Tomorrow, maybe?

Nell stared at the message for a moment before typing her reply. Did she want to see him again, not to pay off her debt to him, but just because she wanted to? Yes, she did.

I'd like to see it. You haven't been there in person for a while, right?

No. But I'm ready to go back. If you wouldn't mind driving one more time?

It wasn't a date. It was just her giving him a ride, like she'd been doing all week. It didn't mean anything, and maybe she'd get some closure, so she could stop thinking about how unhappy he'd looked when she dropped him off this afternoon.

I have to work tomorrow. But I could pick you up after. 4:00?

4:00 will work. Thank you for driving.

It's nothing.

I told you to stop saying that.

She smiled at her phone before typing her reply.

OK. It's not nothing. It is definitely something.

Better. Goodnight, Nell. I'll see you tomorrow.

Goodnight.

She set down the phone and pressed a hand to her sternum, where her pulse raced. Not nothing. Definitely something. The words repeated on a loop in her mind the rest of the evening.

Chapter 8

Ben lifted the blinds and squinted out the window onto his front porch, checking for Nell's car again. He'd asked her to come here again, and drive him on yet another errand, because he hadn't been able to stop himself. And to the clinic, where he hadn't set foot in a month.

There was no need for this impromptu field trip. He was all set to go back to work on Monday, starting with half days. He could handle it now, after this week's outings. Probably.

But he'd had to see her one more time. It hadn't been enough to say goodbye in front of her son, when he couldn't say everything on his mind. Maybe if she saw the clinic, saw how much it meant to him, and how she'd helped bring him back to his work, she'd understand the magnitude of what she'd done for him.

That had been the thought when he'd texted her last night. Now, nerves blasted through him when her battered silver sedan pulled up at the curb. She slid out of the driver's seat and he dropped the blinds.

He checked his suit, smoothing a hand over the vest. Nothing out of place, except his stupid heart, which knocked around his ribcage at the sight of her coming up the drive.

He made himself wait a few beats before opening the door. His brain stopped like it always did around her as she smiled, looking genuinely happy to see him.

He cleared his throat. "Thank you again for coming."

"I'm glad to take you. I have to admit I'm curious about your clinic, now that I've met all your patients."

"I hadn't thought of it, but you have, haven't you?"

She nodded. "And they had nothing but good things to say about you. They all said you're the best."

"I wouldn't go that far," he murmured. She'd replaced her usual outfit with black jeans and a blue polo shirt with a coffee shop logo. "Your other job is at a coffee shop?"

"One day on the weekend, sometimes Saturday and some-times Sunday. My neighbor watches Marco. I didn't have time to change before I came, and okay, that is definitely a coffee stain." She brushed a self-conscious hand over her shirt.

"It's not a problem." He'd made her come all the way out to his house after working a six-day week, and she was worried about her shirt. "But you must be tired. Are you sure you wouldn't rather do this another day?"

She shook her head with a little smile. "I'm here already, anyway. Should we get going? My maps app says it's twenty minutes to downtown. Less traffic on Saturday."

"That sounds about right. I'm ready if you are."

Anxiety didn't even strike him on the short walk to the car, a huge difference from a week ago. Inside the car was another matter, because there were a couple of factors he hadn't anticipated. The car was much smaller than the van, and he was a tall man. He sat much closer to her than he'd been before, their shoulders almost brushing in the small space.

He could smell the coffee shop on her—bitter and toasty, with a sweet hint of caramel or hazelnut syrup layered on top. He shut his eyes and tried not to inhale too deeply.

"Doing okay?" she asked, buckling her seatbelt.

"Yes. Fine."

"Do you want to tell me the address?"

Ben told her, and she programmed it into her phone. "And we're off. I only have an hour or so. I have to go pick up Marco soon."

"Understood." He gripped the door handle, as if that would keep him safe from looking at her too much.

The drive was familiar, but not. It had been so long. New construction had cropped up on the highway, lanes closed that hadn't been before. Even the trees looked different, bursting with pale green early leaves.

"So, you mentioned looking for a third job."

The corner of her mouth turned down. "I don't want a third job, of course. It will mean more time away from Marco. But we need the money."

She put on her turn signal and took the highway exit. "I'm hoping to find something I can do online from home, maybe while he's asleep, or when there's free time."

"I can't imagine you have a lot of free time."

She gave a little laugh. "Not much. But I'll manage. This is a nice part of town."

They'd turned into the older, residential neighborhood that housed the clinic, where restored Victorian homes stood on both sides of quiet, brick streets.

"When I set up the clinic, I wanted it to feel more comfortable, less medical. So we bought a house instead."

"These houses are huge, though."

"They are. Definitely big enough for our needs. The clinic has three floors, with fourteen treatment rooms and three sitting rooms total. I can't imagine it as a family home, but it was, at one point."

Ben's pulse picked up as they got closer. The clinic had been his home away from home, and he hadn't seen it in weeks. His return was due in large part to the woman sitting next to him, and she didn't even realize it.

"This is it." He pointed as she turned down a street lined with Bradford pear trees. Their branches, thick with white blossoms, formed an archway over the brick street.

"Oh. It's so beautiful. With the trees in bloom."

"This is a good time of year to visit. You can park there, in the driveway. There won't be anyone here on a Saturday."

They pulled up to the clinic, and Nell parked next to the hand-painted sign with the clinic's name. His throat tightened at the sight of the familiar building with its slate-blue exterior, white trim, and wraparound porch.

"Thank you for driving. I haven't been in so long."

She put the car in park and turned to face him. "I can already tell, this place is amazing. I'm glad you asked me to come."

Ben took a breath and pulled himself together. "Let me show you around."

Together, they climbed the porch steps. He unlocked the heavy oak door, disarmed the security system, and flipped on the lights of the main reception area. They'd furnished it like an old-fashioned sitting room, with velvet and floral couches, leather armchairs, and stained glass lamps. The reception desk was an old oak rolltop Vanessa had dug up at one of the estate sales she couldn't stay away from.

"This is the main floor reception area. We have sitting rooms on each of the other floors as well."

"It's so homey. It feels like a place people would come to relax. And I love the style." Nell's eyes scanned around them as they walked.

"That's mostly my co-worker Vanessa's doing. She's good at finding vintage furniture and making it all look right together."

He walked down the hallway, flipping on more lights as they went. "These smaller rooms used to be bedrooms, but they've been converted into individual treatment rooms. We have six therapists and two nurses on staff now. But when we started out, it was just me and Vanessa. She's the other senior counselor on staff."

He motioned for her to follow him up a flight of stairs. "My office is on the third floor."

At the top of the staircase, they passed the third-floor reception area and he took out another key to unlock his office. Stepping inside was like going back in time, with everything as he'd left it, from the organized cherrywood desk to the leather couch piled with neutral-toned pillows. Someone had been dusting and watering his plants while he'd been gone.

Behind him, Nell hummed appreciatively. "This is amazing. What a view."

"It's not too bad, right?" The bay windows spanned most of one wall, showing the city skyline and the trees in bloom, pink and white.

He'd never be here, if it hadn't been for her help, and he still hadn't figured out a way to say the words to her. But he had to tell her, to at least let her know a small part of his feelings, if not the whole of them.

Ben turned to face her. She walked the perimeter of his office, studying the walls. She'd folded her arms across her chest, as if trying not to touch anything.

"Is that you?" She squinted at a framed news article on the wall, which included a photo of Ben in a TV studio, shaking the show host's hand.

"Is that *Good Morning USA*?" Her voice rose in disbelief.

He huffed out a laugh. "That was a terrible segment. I was so anxious, I could barely get a word out, even though I'd practiced everything I wanted to say."

She rounded on him. "Are you famous? Like, people know who you are?"

He shook his head. "I doubt that many people know who I am. I wrote some books that got a lot of attention, for a while. I started this clinic. I do speaking engagements. Or at least, I used to. But most people don't follow the psychology world."

"But people who do …"

"Would know who I am, yes." He slid his hands into his pockets, studying her face, which was rapidly changing from surprise to horror.

"Why didn't I know any of that? I could have searched you online, I guess. Maybe I should have. I mean, you bought this place, set up a whole clinic by yourself—"

"I'm so glad you didn't search me." Going by her expression, if she'd known more about him before, that would have been a bad thing.

"You—" She shut her mouth, folded her arms more tightly around herself. "I drove you around all this week, thinking you were someone like me. I mean, it should have been obvious you're not."

Her eyes flicked around the room, refusing to land on his.

"I think we should go back now. I need to get home soon, anyway."

Ben's gut clenched. "What's the matter? Is something wrong?"

"It's nothing. It's fine."

She wasn't fine. Her expression had closed off completely, and she wouldn't look at him.

"Tell me." He took a step closer, panic threading through his veins. She wanted to get away from him. She was going to drop him off, go home, and he'd never see her again. And he still hadn't told her how he felt.

"I helped you because I thought you were like me." Her gaze flashed to his, her voice ragged. "Someone who was going through a hard time, and needed help. But you're not anything like me. I'm a ... a delivery driver. I dropped out of school. And you're ..." She trailed off. "I don't really know you, do I?"

"You do know me. Better than anyone." His voice came out low and sharp. He took another step closer. She'd backed into the door frame of his office, and he stepped into her personal space. He was too close, close enough to smell her hair, and he should really back away now, but his body wasn't listening to the demands of his brain. His hand clenched into a fist at his side, aching to reach for her.

"I *was* just someone who needed help. I had all this." He waved a hand, indicating his office. "I had all these accomplishments, and I was broken, and a mess, and everything was wrong inside me. And the only time I felt right in all the last year was the time I spent with you." His voice cracked on the last word, and he swallowed.

She looked shell-shocked. He gazed into the storm of her eyes—confusion and sadness, a hint of longing—and the rest

89

of whatever he was going to say disappeared from his mind.

"Ben." She choked out the word and flung her arms around his waist in a fierce hug, burying her face in his chest. "I'm sorry. I shouldn't have said those things."

His eyes slid shut at the feel of her pressed against him, his arms going around her tightly. He pressed his face into her hair, let himself inhale the coffee shop smell, and underneath, the scent of her citrus shampoo and her skin, powerful as any drug.

She turned her face up to him and without thinking, he put his mouth on hers, because he had to, because he couldn't not do it. Her response was immediate and strong. She wrapped her arms around his neck and kissed him back, opening her mouth under his and threading her hands into his hair.

Ben's brain shut off and he pressed his body against the length of hers, chasing more of her coffee and caramel taste. A flush rose up his chest, pulse thundering in his ears. He was lost, drunk on the best feeling he'd felt in forever.

Her knees buckled and he caught her waist, bracing her against the door frame. His hands slid up, under the hem of her shirt, palming the smooth skin of her lower back. She was too soft to be real, delicious under his fingers.

She gasped and pulled her mouth from his, and he dropped his head, gulping in deep breaths.

He hadn't meant to kiss her, and there was a reason he wasn't supposed to do it, but for the life of him, he couldn't think of what it was right now. Nothing about that had been wrong or bad. Except how desperate he'd gotten, and how quickly he'd gotten there.

He'd pushed her against a wall and shoved his hands under her clothes, not something he'd normally do with a first kiss, and it had been so good, like he'd been starving for months and someone had set a meal in front of him.

But she'd stopped, and he'd respect that. He took a measured step backward. She leaned against the doorframe, staring up at him, her pupils dilated.

"I …" He cleared his throat. Tried again. "Can we sit down for a minute?"

She nodded and followed him to the couch. Once they were sitting side by side, he remembered the reason, the very good and sensible reason, why he shouldn't have kissed her.

"You don't date." His voice was wrecked. The end of the sentence came out sounding like a question.

"I don't. I haven't, not once since I got divorced. I have a rule." She touched her fingers to her mouth, as if remembering the kiss.

"I'm sure you have good reasons for the rule."

"I did. I do." She turned to face him, her expression conflicted. "But I liked kissing you."

A shiver went through him. "I liked it too."

A little smile turned the corner of her mouth up. "I could kind of tell. But we can't. It's not a good idea for me."

"I'm not trying to change your mind. But I would like to know why."

He'd expected her to pull away from him at that, but instead, she reached out and put a hand on top of his, where it rested between them on the couch.

"Are you sure you want to hear this?"

He might not want to hear it, if the story involved her getting hurt. But she deserved for someone to hear it. It was one thing he could do for her.

"I'm a very good listener."

Chapter 9

The problem with opening up to someone a little bit was that it led to telling them even more. The parts of herself she'd guarded so carefully were about to be exposed, but after that kiss, it didn't seem like such a big deal anymore.

She'd hugged Ben on impulse, and she definitely hadn't meant to kiss him, but there was no denying her reaction, not with aftershocks still shivering through her. If they ever did more than that, she might not survive it.

She'd found him attractive from the start, but there'd been no connection between that feeling and the idea anything could happen between them in real life. He was off limits, like all men. She'd wanted to help him. But maybe she'd also just … wanted him.

And now she was about to tell him the story she hadn't told anyone before, because after Mom died, there'd been no one to tell it to. There were reasons she'd avoided this conversation, hadn't let herself say the words aloud. This would hurt. After years of being mostly numb, she'd let herself feel something, and this was the result.

"I'm not sure where to start." She paused, took a breath, and felt Ben's fingers contract, giving her hand a light squeeze. "You already know I left school to get married, after Mom died."

"Yes, we talked about that part." Ben stayed quiet, letting her pick through the words she wanted to say next.

"When I didn't have Mom anymore, I was kind of lost. I was twenty-one, but still a kid in a lot of ways. I felt like an orphan. I barely made it to any of my classes that semester, my grades were awful, and I had no social life. I'd worked so hard to get to college, because I wanted to make her proud. And she was. So proud of me. Then she was gone, and I couldn't figure out why I was doing any of it."

Ben nodded. "Understandable. You were grieving."

"I was, but I didn't realize how much it would affect every part of my life. I didn't know how long the process would take, either. When I met Kurt—my ex-husband—I was directionless. And he took charge of everything. He made it easy, because I didn't have to make any decisions. He decided everything, and I could just do what he said."

"Decisions about what?" Ben's tone remained mild, but he sat up straighter next to her.

"About everything. But mostly small stuff at first. Where we went to dinner, what clothes I wore. When I enrolled for the next semester, he helped me pick my classes. I thought it was nice at first. That it showed how much he cared for me."

She took a deep inhale. "But he also criticized me a lot. I never did anything well enough for him. I was late, or clumsy, or my hair was messy, or I didn't clean my dorm room enough.

Like I said, little stuff at first."

Ben's brows came down. "He's the one who made you think bad things about yourself. The other day, when you said you don't have any skills. That's where that came from."

She nodded. "I guess, when someone criticizes you all the time, part of you starts to believe it. Anyway, he was the one who told me to quit school. He said my grades were bad, and I couldn't focus, so why not stop? So I did what he said. I was so stupid."

"You were not," Ben said, his tone heated. "You were doing the best you could, while someone took advantage of your weakness."

"I didn't think of it like that."

"I'm sorry. I didn't mean to interrupt you. But I can't let you call yourself stupid in the context of this story."

No one had ever stood up for her. Not back then, and not since. The fact that Ben was standing up for the past version of her soothed some of the ache of reliving the memory. And he was angry, yes, but angry on her behalf. He'd never take out his anger on her, and that gave her the courage to keep going.

"Anyway. He said a degree wouldn't help me out much anyway. He wanted to work and take care of me and our kids. And I did want a family. So much. I missed Mom, and I thought starting a family of my own should be my priority. It made sense at the time. But I was so naive. Why didn't I see what was happening?"

He squeezed her hand again. "None of us are good at seeing our lives from the outside."

She kept her gaze straight ahead, because if she looked at him now, she might not get through the next part.

"Dropping out wasn't even the lowest point. A few months

after we got married, I found out I'm infertile. We'd been trying for a baby, and when I didn't get pregnant, I went to the doctor for some tests. I ... I don't know if you want to hear the next part."

"I want to hear it, if you want to tell me."

Nell pulled her hand out of his and turned to face him on the couch. "I want you to know the reason why I am how I am now. Not because we're dating or anything. God, I don't think you'd want that from me, after I lay all this on you. But we've gotten to know each other this week, and with what just happened ..."

Ben's expression turned pained. "We can talk more about that later. But I want to know."

She folded her arms over her chest. "The night when Kurt came home from work and I told him I couldn't have a baby ... I'd never seen him like that. He changed, right in front of me. Or maybe I just realized how he was for the first time. He yelled at me. Punched a hole in the wall. He didn't hit me, but I was so scared. I didn't recognize him. He said ... He said he was sorry he married me. And that I was worthless to him now."

Ben was listening with his whole body, but he didn't interrupt the flow of her words. His hands clenched into fists on his thighs, the knuckles white.

"And I was so young and stupid, I tried to make it better with him. I thought if I could get on his good side again, smooth everything over, we could get back to how we used to be in our relationship. Not that it was ever good. I know that now."

"I don't know how I did it, but I convinced him we could be happy if we adopted a child. I still wanted a baby so much. Marco was twelve months old when we adopted him. I just ... I fell in love with him the minute I met him. When the adoption process went through, I knew I was the luckiest person in the world to be his mom. But not Kurt. He was never the same. He just got colder and meaner. And then one day he left. I haven't seen him since."

Nell wrapped her arms so tightly around her middle, her ribs ached. She didn't look at Ben, because he would probably be wearing that kind, compassionate expression on his face, and then she'd cry, in front of him this time. Which could not happen.

"Sweetheart, I am so sorry." Ben didn't seem to notice the endearment had slipped out. "I'm sorry he treated you like that."

"It's okay."

"It's not. But it does help me understand."

"The worst part is, I feel so guilty. I brought Marco into our lives when our marriage was so bad. And I worry all the time that if I don't keep everything together, someone will take him away from me."

There it was. Her worst fear, right out in the open.

"They can't do that. Unless you're neglecting him, which you clearly are not."

"Really?" She let herself meet his eyes for the first time since starting the whole terrible story.

"Really. We have a family counselor on staff who works with cases like this. You are not going to lose Marco. I can even set up an appointment with her, if you want to talk to her about it."

She took a shuddering inhale, relief piercing her chest. "Thank you. I swear, I've worried the most about that."

"Can I please hug you now?"

She gave an aborted little nod, and Ben's arm came around her, pulling her close to his side. His hand smoothed up and down her arm. With the truth out in the open, the heaviness of her past lost some of its grip.

"Nell. What happened to you isn't your fault." Ben paused for a minute, seeming to choose his words. "That was an abusive relationship. You know that, right?"

She looked down at her lap. "Yes. Of course I know that now."

"So you aren't to blame. Not for any of your feelings, or any of the ways you've coped with it since then."

"I guess I know that, too." She spread her fingers over the leather upholstery next to her thigh. "This couch ... It's magical, right? It makes people tell you things."

He huffed out a laugh. "This is my therapy couch. But I promise you, I don't hold any of my patients like this. Or kiss them."

"That's a good thing." Nell put her hand on his forearm, feeling the warm muscle beneath his sleeve jump under her fingertips. "About that kiss ... You can see why I haven't dated. I didn't trust myself to not mess things up again. I couldn't take the chance."

"I do see why."

"And I think that's why I had a bad reaction, earlier. To finding out those things I hadn't known about you before. I don't think I'm very trusting anymore."

"Understandable."

"So you probably don't want to get involved with me now."

"I want ..." Ben shifted to look down at her. His face was so close, she could kiss him again, and she wanted that. The feel of his mouth, the warmth of his lean body pressed against her.

It had only been a taste, and she wanted more. She froze in shock at her own thought train, pinned by his eyes.

"I want whatever we can have together," he said. "I want to know you. You already know I'm far from perfect myself."

She frowned, drawing away from him. "But you're smart and successful. And kind of famous."

"And I've only left the house a handful of times in the last month. All of them with you. Thank you for that, by the way."

"But it's not your fault. You have anxiety. A lot of people have it."

He shook his head, as if he didn't quite believe her. "I've known I had anxiety my entire adult life, and I still let it get this bad. But I've changed my medication dose, and you've helped me get back out the door. It's just … I can't figure out why. Why I wasn't able to get it under control this time. Which means it could happen again. I'm sorry. I don't usually sit on this couch and tell other people my problems."

"But you do with me."

The corner of his mouth twisted up. "Only with you, it seems."

"So … What should we do?"

He was quiet for a moment before he spoke again. "I can't tell you what to do. But whenever a patient in my practice starts a new medication, we do a three-week trial run to see if it's going to work, or if we need to adjust the dosage, or try a different medicine. Most of the time, we don't know if it's going to work until we give it three weeks."

"The medicine takes that long to work?"

"It does. And I'm wondering if the same might be true for us. We'd have to try dating to know if it works for either of us."

"And if it doesn't work out?"

"We'd part ways. No obligations."

Would it be any easier to say goodbye to him in three weeks? Things could only get more complicated, more messy. But she'd shown him parts of her past no one had seen, and he hadn't run away screaming. He'd said he wanted to know her.

"I might be willing to try it, except for Marco. I don't want him getting confused. Thinking we're together when we're not. It would be too hard for him when … if it doesn't work out."

"We could tell him we're friends. It does seem like it would be smarter not to tell him at first."

"I can't risk hurting him." Nell stood in a rush. "I'm sorry, Ben. I don't think I can."

Ben gave a sad little nod, looking up at her from the couch. "I understand. It was just an idea. A way of thinking about it. But you've been through a lot, and I'm not very functional right now, either. Maybe neither one of us is ready to date."

He shoved a hand through his glossy black hair with its threads of silver, the waves uncharacteristically messy because she'd had her hands in them twenty minutes ago.

Of course he was as worried as she was about dating. He'd shared as much of his own vulnerabilities, maybe more than she had. He needed patience and understanding as much as she did.

She'd stepped closer to him without realizing it. She stood right between his knees, and he looked up at her, brown eyes soft and sad in his sharp, severe-looking face.

She cupped his jaw in her hands and pressed her mouth to his, because she couldn't resist, softer and much gentler than their earlier kiss. Ben's lips parted on an indrawn breath. He'd kept his eyes open, and they drew her in, asking her to trust him, telling her it would be all right.

She pulled back a couple of inches. "If we did do this trial run, would you kiss me? As part of the three weeks?"

His expression darkened, pupils widening. "I want to. Unless you say no. Then I would absolutely respect that boundary."

"Okay." She pulled in a breath, straightened. "Let's try one evening together. Maybe have dinner. We can see how it goes. Then I'll make a decision."

Where this calm, authoritative person had come from, she didn't know. But it was her decision to make. At every step, he'd let her lead the way, never pushing her to do what she didn't want.

Ben swallowed. "One date. I can do that. The, uh … Dinner might have to be at my house or yours. I'm not sure about going to restaurants yet." He dropped his eyes, looking sheepish.

"Neither one of us has to apologize for what we need. Because it's not our fault. That's what you told me."

"I guess I did."

"Good, then." Nell held out a hand to him, and he took it and stood. She glanced at her watch and didn't even panic at the time. "I have to get back now. I'm supposed to pick up Marco in fifteen minutes."

"Nell, thank you for trying this with me. Even if it doesn't work out, I want you to know, I'll never treat you like you were treated before."

"I know." She flashed him a smile, because she did know that much. She might not trust this would work out, or that he wouldn't hurt her without meaning to. But he would never do it on purpose, never be cruel. And that was enough for now.

Ben held her hand in the car the whole way back to his house. He promised to text her to set up their date. Before he got out of the car, he brought her hand to his lips, brushing his mouth over her knuckles. At the old-fashioned gesture, she shivered, fighting the urge to pull him closer for another kiss.

He lifted his face to hers, eyes glittering almost black. "I'll talk to you soon."

"Okay." Her voice sounded breathless to her own ears.

He walked at a brisk pace up the steps to his house, and she watched him go. He'd removed his jacket and slung it over one shoulder, and his walk was lighter, easier than she'd ever seen. A beautiful man, so stern and reserved, but he let her see his flaws and conflicts too. He'd let himself need her.

It was one date. Maybe three weeks of dating. She had choices now, when she'd never had any choices before. And she'd choose to try.

Chapter 10

Ben's phone rang three times in a row with his work ringtone at 6:45 a.m. on Monday. The repeating sound dragged him off the treadmill and into the kitchen, where the device buzzed on the counter. He frowned at Vanessa's name on the screen and swiped right.

"What's going on?"

"Ben. Thank God you picked up." Vanessa pitched her voice low, whispering into the speaker of her phone. "We have a situation."

"What happened? And what are you doing there before 7:00?"

"I always get here early on Mondays. And it's about Penny. Your patient? When I got here, she was sitting on the porch steps. She looked like she was about to fall off them, though. I asked her if she had an appointment with you, but she wouldn't say anything. All she would say was she was waiting for you, and I haven't gotten a word out of her since then."

"What? I didn't arrange to meet with her there. We had a

video appointment scheduled for later this afternoon."

He'd scheduled two in-person appointments this morning, at the carefully chosen times of 10:00 and 11:00. Afterward, he'd planned to come back home. Two hours in the office would already stretch his limited capacity.

"I thought you wouldn't have a meeting this early. I said I'd call and check with you, and I got her to come inside. She's … not looking well."

"Symptoms? Pupils dilated? Rapid pulse?"

"No, and no. No signs of concussion or a stroke. It's more like she's half-asleep, to be honest. I can't get her to speak."

He shoved a hand through his hair. "Is there anyone from her family we can call? Her file should have next of kin listed."

"I checked, and it's only her son listed there."

"Damn. He's in college in California. That's no help."

Ben was already jogging up the steps to his bedroom. Inside, he yanked a suit out of the closet and tossed it on the bed. He toed off his sneakers and grabbed a towel off the rack in the bathroom.

"I almost called an ambulance, right before you picked up," Vanessa whispered. "But you know she'll get dumped into the ER, sit there all day, and they'll send her home with god knows what meds. We'll never figure out what happened."

"Don't call them yet, as long as her vitals are normal. Emergency services aren't set up to deal with our patients."

"I'll do whatever you tell me to do. I just need some instructions."

"I'm coming in. I'll be there in thirty minutes. Keep checking her pulse and call EMS if it drops below sixty."

He clicked off the call and jumped into the shower. This wasn't how he'd planned to return to work today. He'd already been dreading the curious stares of coworkers and patients after his long absence. Now he'd be in the office for upwards of five hours, instead of two, and with an emergency situation, too.

His pulse spiked, and didn't slow as he dressed in his full armor—black wool suit with a royal blue tie, blue pocket square, and his platinum tie pin.

Fifteen minutes later, he stood by the front door, ready and not ready to go. He patted his pockets. Keys, phone, wallet. Now, to get into his own car and drive himself to work, like he used to do every single day without a thought.

He'd do this because it was the right thing to do, because he was needed, and people depended on him. And also because Nell would be happy for him. Her sunny smile appeared in his mind and he held onto the image as he twisted the door handle.

She believed he could do this, so he would. Tomorrow night, on their first date, he'd tell her about it.

The few steps to his car were quick and focused. He slid into the driver's seat and slammed the door shut. Instinct would kick in as soon as he started driving. He couldn't have forgotten how in the last month.

The drive downtown passed in a blur. His brain and hands remembered the route, and he pulled into his reserved parking space behind the clinic and killed the ignition. A few more deep breaths with his hands on the wheel. The panic hadn't arrived yet—not while walking to his car, and not while driving. But panic attacks were sneaky bastards that liked to tackle you from behind.

He caught sight of himself in the rearview mirror as he opened the car door. From the outside, he appeared as he always had. Calm and in control. He locked the car and jogged up the clinic steps.

In the main sitting room, Penny slumped over the couch arm. Vanessa perched on the edge of a nearby armchair, and when he came in the door, she jumped up and strode toward him. Her long floral skirt swished around her ankles, her auburn hair a voluminous cloud around her face.

She smiled at him and pulled him into a quick hug.

"It's so good to see you, despite the circumstances. I missed you."

He cleared his throat, thumped her awkwardly on the back. "I missed you, too." He glanced over her shoulder at Penny. "Has she said anything else?"

"No. She's been like this for almost an hour now."

"Will you block off this area of the clinic? Have the first patients come in the side door and use the second floor sitting room as a waiting area for the morning."

"Of course. I'll make a sign for the front door." She hurried to lock the front door and headed down the hall to the side entrance.

Ben crossed the room and knelt by the sofa in front of Penny. The older woman's eyes looked dull, unfocused, her expression free of any spark of her usual personality. She'd put her shirt on backward, too. She'd been doing so well last week, when he'd seen her on their video call.

"Penny, can you hear me?" he asked.

At the sound of his voice, her eyes shifted in his direction. The pupils moved in slow motion, as if on a delay.

"Dr. Friedman?" she asked, her voice thick and slow.

"Yes, it's me. I heard you came in to see me this morning."

"I thought we had an appointment. But I ... couldn't

remember when. I wanted to be on time."

"You were on time. No need to worry." He kept his voice light.

"Oh. That's good."

"Can I sit next to you?" He stood slowly, not wanting to startle her.

"Yesss." She drew the word out, frowning at the sound of it. "Something isn't right. I don't feel normal. I needed to tell you. You said … If something went wrong, I'd know who to ask."

"That's exactly right, to ask for help. Do you know when you took your last dose of your antidepressant?" He spoke slowly, making sure she understood the words.

"Last night. Before bed, like always."

"Good. Perfect. And did you do anything else, anything different from your normal routine?"

She shook her head in slow motion, then nodded. "I had a doctor appointment with my regular doctor yesterday. He gave me a new medicine."

The hair on the back of Ben's neck stood up. "What was the medicine for?"

"For muscle spasms. I told him my legs had been twitching at night. I took a picture of the bottle."

With a shaking hand, she unlocked her phone and handed him the device, showing him a photo of her new prescription.

As the words on the label registered, Ben stopped himself from swearing, but the urge was strong. His own hand shook as he handed the phone back to her, part adrenaline and part his old friend, anxiety.

He placed a gentle hand on her shoulder. "Penny, I think you're having a reaction to taking two medicines that don't mix well together. Your antidepressant doesn't work well with the new medicine."

She turned her face to him, tears sliding down her cheeks. "Am I going to be okay? Did I do something wrong?"

"You're going to be fine. This isn't an emergency, but it is serious. You didn't do anything wrong. But we need to get you to the hospital so they can monitor you while the medicine wears off. I'll have one of our nurses drive you there. You should stop taking that new medicine. I'll call your doctor and discuss it with him."

"Okay."

He held out a hand to help her stand, and looked her in the eye. "I'm glad you told me. You made sure someone knew things weren't right."

He didn't want to think about her driving here in this state. She was lucky she'd come before 7:00, when there wasn't much traffic.

"Thank you, Doctor."

"Wait here, and I'll get Sophie to help you out." He moved calmly, as if everything was under control. But as soon as he cleared the door of the sitting room, he sped into action. Vanessa waited for him in the hallway.

"We need Sophie," he said. "She'll drive Penny to the ER for a vitals check, wait with her while they monitor symptoms, then drive her home."

"What was it? Did she tell you?"

"Drug interaction. Her doctor prescribed her a muscle relaxant and didn't check her other meds."

"Son of a bitch," Vanessa hissed. "It would have taken them two minutes to check."

"I had to restrain myself from saying the same thing in front of her. He could have prescribed her anything. Sleep aids would have been a disaster. This could have been so much worse. As it is, the meds she took should wear off in a couple of hours. As soon as I get upstairs, I'll put in a call to her doctor. And try not to raise my voice."

"I say, raise it. Who the hell do they think they are? She'll be okay, though?" Vanessa asked.

"Yes, I think so. But I want them monitoring her heart rate for a couple of hours. And I want Sophie there to tell them what meds she took."

"I'll get her." Vanessa disappeared in a swish of skirts.

Ben sagged against the wall in the hallway. As the adrenaline wore off, his hands continued to shake, and he shoved them in his pockets. The sheer effort to come here had eaten away at his energy reserves. He had no stamina for the real world.

But another part of him thrummed to life, the part that had forgotten what it felt like to help someone in need. This was what he was supposed to be doing. This place was his, and the patients counted on him. He hadn't been giving them everything he could. But you couldn't pour from an empty cup.

He watched from the window as Penny got into Sophie's car. He'd given the nurse a written note explaining the situation to give to the ER doctors. After they pulled away from the clinic's parking lot, he went upstairs to his office.

Cameron, Ben's administrative assistant, sat at his desk in the reception area outside Ben's office, head bent over his laptop, wearing his usual suspenders and bowtie. He startled, eyes widening, as Ben appeared.

"Ben. You're early." To his credit, Cameron didn't stare. The younger man, a grad school student, was used to unusual events at the clinic.

"I am. Bit of an emergency. You're here early, too." Was everyone at the clinic working longer hours, or was it his imagination?

"Mondays are always hectic. I heard a patient showed up here at 6:30 today." Cameron glanced at his computer screen. "Your first appointment isn't until 10:00, but let me know if you need anything. There's already a water bottle on your desk."

"Got it. Thank you. I'll be in my office."

That sounded self-assured enough. Ben went into his office and shut the door. He sank into the chair behind his desk and scanned the room.

The last time he'd sat on the couch had been with Nell, two days ago. He had a ridiculous urge to call her and hear her voice. But that would be too much, too soon. They weren't dating. It could wait until tomorrow.

He booted up his laptop and pulled up Penny's patient records, getting to work.

After his second in-person appointment left for the day, Vanessa poked her head in the door.

"Okay to come in for a sec?"

"Of course."

She shut the door behind her. "I wanted to let you know they discharged Penny from the hospital, and Sophie got her settled in at home. She's doing fine."

"Great news. Thank you for your help this morning, by the way."

"Of course. It was just like old times."

"Just like old times," he echoed, smoothing a hand down his vest. He'd been here over five hours now.

She examined his face. "How are you holding up? Doing

okay?"

"I'm fine." He waved a hand dismissively.

"You're not fine. But since you won't tell me what's going on, I'm using my powers of observation."

"And they're telling you …"

"They're telling me you're exhausted. This morning took a lot out of you."

"Maybe a little."

She made a frustrated sound. "Fine. I'm never going to hear about it. Don't tell me anything about your personal life. I'm only one of your oldest friends, and your business partner, too. But go home and rest this afternoon, yeah?"

"That's the plan. But I'll be back tomorrow. Two morning appointments a day this week."

"You're really back." She let out a long breath. "Thank God."

"Did you hear anything more after they finished the flower deliveries last week?"

"People loved the flowers. We got a lot of thank-you cards and phone calls. But also … A couple more patients left the practice last week."

Ben straightened in his chair. "What happened? Did they say why?"

"You're not going to believe it."

"Try me."

"The other clinic—Harmonious Mind—ran an ad on social media comparing themselves to us."

"I'm sorry, they did what?"

"They called us out by name. Their ad said, 'If you like The Well Space, but don't like their prices, give us a try.'"

Ben shoved his chair back and stood. "They'll get what they pay for."

"That was my thought, too. That's why I had Cameron reach out to a few of our patients."

Ben's gaze sharpened on her. "And tell them what, exactly?"

Vanessa folded her arms across her chest, a smirk on her face. "Oh, we didn't ask them to say anything about the ad specifically, of course. We just asked if they'd post photos of themselves holding their flower arrangements, and tag us. To show our personal touch."

"I see." His stomach clenched. This was the exact reason he needed to be here. A personal touch meant in-person appointments, not video calls. The flowers were a good start, but he needed to be here, not half days, but full days.

"I'm going to brainstorm other things we can do to bring people back," he said. "And I owe you flowers, too. For keeping things going while I was gone. I promise, I'll be around more now."

She flashed him a huge smile from the door. "Roses are my favorite. Now, go home before you fall over."

Chapter 11

Ben arrived at Nell's house for their dinner date with a bottle of wine and a bag of rocks. She'd said Marco liked the geode, so he'd brought a few others, just in case.

Her house was part of a short row of attached rental townhomes. The chipped gray exterior paint could use a touchup, and it appeared no one had mowed the lawn yet this spring. The grass had grown to ankle height, and weeds lined the sidewalk.

Her front door opened and she greeted him with a smile. She was barefoot, wearing dark jeans and a white T-shirt, her usual high ponytail swinging as she walked down the path to meet him. He'd never seen anything more beautiful.

"You found us," she said.

"It wasn't too hard." He shut the car door and locked it with the fob.

Her eyes widened as she took him in. "You're not wearing a suit."

"I do own other clothing. Mostly, I wear suits for work." He'd chosen the white button-down and black pants in the hopes he'd look more relaxed.

"Well, I've never seen you not wearing a suit." She ushered him in the front door. "You look good this way."

"You look nice, too." His eyes caught hers and held, and he was right back where he'd been on Saturday. Tongue-tied, and a few seconds away from kissing her.

Footsteps thundered down the steps, and Marco skidded around the corner. He stared at Ben for a long moment, then directed a meaningful look at Nell.

"Marco wants us to show you what we found at the park on Sunday. Marco, I'm going to show Ben around the house first. Then, we'll show him your rocks. Do you want to go up and get them?"

Marco rolled his eyes, turned, and ran back up the steps.

Nell gave a little laugh. "He's so excited to show you these rocks we found. But I don't have the heart to take them into the rock shop and cut them in half. What if there's nothing inside them? He'll be so disappointed."

Ben's chest tightened. "He wanted to look for rocks?"

"He didn't talk about anything else for two days."

"I brought more to show him." He held up the bag. "I hope you don't mind."

"Of course not. He'll be thrilled." She took the bag and the wine bottle and set them on the dining table, which was covered with a dinosaur-print tablecloth. Ben scanned the small room. Plants covered one half of the dining table. More plants lined the windowsill and hung from hooks on the ceiling. A brief glance into her small kitchen revealed greenery in tiny pots on the countertops. In the corner of the dining room stood a couple of the pots they'd taken from the hardware store last week.

"They weren't dead." He tipped his head in the direction of the plastic pots, sitting on the floor by the window. The formerly dried-out husks now sported dozens of new leaves.

She flashed him a brilliant smile. "I told you they weren't dead. Just under-watered and too much sun. But I fixed them up."

"You're a plant doctor."

"A little bit." She went to the table and picked up a small succulent. "This one is Matilda. She's a jade plant. She only had two leaves when I got her."

"You name your plants?" A smile threatened the corners of Ben's mouth.

"Of course. It helps them grow and it makes them feel special."

"That makes a lot of sense. And Matilda is a good name."

"My mom loved old-fashioned names. That's how I ended up with the name Penelope. So easy to spell for a kid." She rolled her eyes. "But I like giving them names my mom would have liked. It reminds me of her."

"The ficus plant you gave me. I thought it came from the shop. But was it one of yours, from your collection?"

"It was one of mine. I thought you needed it."

Because it was like him. Neglected and in need of someone who understood it. God, she'd thought he needed fixing up, like one of her dying plants. And there it was again, that feeling she saw the real him, even when nobody else did, and she accepted him.

He held her gaze. "I did need it. And I didn't even know." He cleared his throat. "And does my ficus have a name?"

"I don't want to tell you. You'll laugh at me."

"I promise not to laugh."

She shifted her eyes away from his. "It's Hortense."

"Hortense is the perfect name for it. Her."

Her smile was blinding, one of the real ones. "I knew you'd get it."

She gestured over his shoulder to the hallway behind him. "Well, I'll give you a quick tour. Won't take long. Kitchen and dining room are here, obviously. The living room's straight ahead."

He followed her back to the small living area, which held a well-used gray couch, worn carpet, a TV on a wooden table, and several dozen more plants, none of which he could identify. A few framed pencil sketches hung on the wall, pictures of rioting gardens full of blooms and greenery.

"Did you draw these?" he asked.

"Oh. Yeah, I did, in college. My wild landscape design plans." She waved a dismissive hand at them.

"They're really good." The sketches had a fairytale quality, showing winding paths, archways choked with flowering vines, and ivy-covered walls.

"I'm a terrible artist. But they're what I imagined when I planned my dream gardens. Anyway. Upstairs are two bedrooms and another bathroom. It's not as … It's nothing fancy."

"It's perfect. Thank you for having me over. When I asked you out, I didn't mean to make you cook. This isn't a very normal date." He rubbed the back of his neck, thinking of his rare past dates, at expensive restaurants and the theater. She deserved that much, and more.

"I like cooking. Anyway, we're just trying things out, right?"

"Right." If they did this again, if she agreed to the three-week trial run idea, he'd invite her over to his house. Maybe even attempt to go out.

Marco's head appeared over the railing of the staircase.

"You can bring them down," Nell called up to him.

Marco carried a canvas tote bag down the steps, hoisting the heavy weight up onto the coffee table. He looked up at Ben, his expectations clear.

"Ben brought some rocks to show you, too," she said.

"I did, but I want to see what you found, first. Did you go to the park to look for them?" Ben asked.

Marco nodded. He reached into the bag and pulled out tissue paper-wrapped bundles.

"He wanted to roll them up in paper. So they wouldn't hit one another and break," Nell explained.

"That was very smart." Ben reached for the first rock and unrolled it out of the paper wrapping. "Should we take a look?"

Marco nodded. A few minutes later, they'd unwrapped all the rocks and laid them out on the table in front of them. Ben picked up each one and turned it over, examining it. Some of them were solid rock. But a couple of them were geodes.

He smiled at Marco. "I think you've got a couple with crystals inside." Marco's eyes lit up. "Look at this one. It's round, like a golf ball. You looked for that shape, right?"

Marco nodded vigorously.

Ben met Nell's eyes. She raised an eyebrow, a silent question, and Ben gave her a quick nod of confirmation.

"M-mom says we might not be able to go to the rock store this week." Marco said, folding his arms across his chest. He scowled up at his mother. "I d-d-don't …" Words failed him, and he pressed his lips together again.

116

"I'll take you soon, I promise," Nell reassured him. "I thought Ben should take a look at them first."

"You didn't believe me. I told you they were geodes," Marco said, clearly holding a grudge.

"You have a good eye," he told Marco. "We can never be sure until we check, but I feel pretty certain you found some."

"I t-told her that."

"It was your first time looking, though. I'm sure your mom wanted me to double check."

Marco's face brightened. "Because you're an expert?"

Ben shook his head, smiling. "I'm no expert, but I do have experience. Would you like to see some of the other crystals I brought?"

"Yes. Where are they?"

"In the dining room," Nell said. "If you get them and bring them back here, I'll finish off dinner."

Thirty minutes later, Ben was surrounded by rocks, with a very excited boy leaning over his shoulder. Marco's difficulty speaking had evaporated. He peppered Ben with questions about where he'd found the rocks, how to pronounce their names, and where the rock and gem store was, so his mom could take him there.

He glanced up to see Nell standing in the doorway to the living room, a strange expression on her face.

"Dinner's all ready. If you guys want to come eat."

Marco hopped off the couch. "My mom makes good food. You'll like it." He raced down the hall to the kitchen, leaving them alone.

"Thanks for bringing the rocks," Nell said, her tone soft.

"I had no idea they would be so popular."

"He really found some geodes?"

"Yes, I'm pretty sure. I'll give you the address of the gem shop. They don't charge much to cut them open."

They ate dinner—chicken parmesan and pasta—surrounded by plants at the little table, with Marco chattering about dinosaurs and fossils. This wasn't like any date Ben had been on before, and he never would have planned anything like this in his former life. But it was what he'd needed. To feel a part of something, to feel like he belonged.

Nell smiled at him across the table, another of her genuine smiles. What if she'd gone to someone else's porch, that first day? What if their paths had never crossed? He'd be sitting alone in his house tonight.

After dinner, he helped her with the dishes while Marco watched TV. Then they wrapped up Marco's rocks, and Ben put away the rocks he'd brought with him. Nell ushered Marco upstairs to take a bath, and the sounds of running water drifted down from above. Ben waited on the couch, and she came back downstairs a half hour later.

"I got him tucked into bed, but it might take him a while to fall asleep. Exciting evening." She settled onto the couch next to him.

Ben wouldn't sleep either, but for other reasons, his body humming with life and warmth. He wanted to burst out her door and run for miles. He wanted to grab her and kiss her until neither of them could breathe.

Nell leaned back against the couch cushions, turning her head to look at him. Up close, the different shades of gray in her eyes shifted in the low light, and he let himself fall into staring at them, spiraling deeper into his fantasies.

With effort, he pulled his gaze away, before he forgot what he'd meant to tell her tonight.

"I did a bit of research on something. I don't want you to feel obligated to use the information, though. If it's not useful, ignore it."

"Okay." She frowned, pulling back a few inches. "What is it?"

"The other day, you mentioned you were the first person in your family to attend college. I looked into the University of Missouri's scholarship programs, and they have several scholarships for first generation college students."

"Oh. I … That's very nice of you to look it up. I didn't know." She folded her arms over her chest and looked out the window, at the dying sunlight. "But even if money wasn't an issue, I don't have the time. With all my jobs, and taking care of Marco. When would I go to class?"

"I understand. I know it might not work for you, and I'm not trying to talk you into it. But I can text you the link if you want it."

"Okay. It's been a long time since I thought about finishing school. I always thought of it as something far-off in the future. But it's been seven years already."

"You'll know when it's time to take the leap. And speaking of taking leaps, I went into the clinic yesterday, and again today."

She sat up straighter. "You really did?"

"Yes, a patient had a health crisis yesterday. And I got in the car and drove there."

"And you were okay? No panic attack?"

"None. I was a lot more tired than usual afterward. I went home at noon. But I'm going to start working half days in the clinic again."

"That's amazing news. It sounds dumb to say I'm proud of you, but I'm proud of you."

"I couldn't have done it without you."

She shook her head. "Of course you could. You would have left your house eventually, with me or not."

"No. It wasn't just that you got me out of the house. It was … I can't explain it. I knew I could tell you about it later, like this. That I'd have someone to tell."

I pictured your face to help me be strong. Ben closed his mouth, before the full admission came out.

"I did it because it was the right thing to do," he said after a moment. "But also because it was the thing I knew you would want me to do."

She shook her head. "Don't say that. That's not … I don't deserve the credit for your progress."

"I'm giving it to you."

"I wish you wouldn't." She covered her face with her hands in embarrassment.

He put a hand on her upper arm, finally touching her like he'd been aching to do all evening. With a gentle pull, he tugged her closer to him on the couch and folded his arm around her. Her head rested on his shoulder as if it was meant to be in that spot.

"Nell. I realized something. You might not already know these things, so I have to make sure I say the words. I think you're the most amazing, beautiful, kind person I've—"

The rest of his words were cut off when she turned and kissed him, hard and messy. He kissed her back, drowning in the feel of it, his hands cupping her face to hold her there. He could go on like this for hours, and it wouldn't be enough. He would never get enough of her.

She made a frustrated sound and pushed her torso closer, not breaking the kiss. He hauled her onto his lap, her legs draped sideways across his, exactly where she was supposed to be, her weight on him sweet and warm. His hand slid up her back, under the thin T-shirt, needing more contact, more of her skin.

She had the top two buttons of his shirt undone, her hands roaming under the collar, when a click at the top of the staircase made her startle and break away from him. She slid off his lap in a rush.

"It's Marco. The bathroom door." She was out of breath, her lips glossy and swollen. Strands of hair had escaped her ponytail. She stared across at him, still breathing hard.

"Right." Once again, his brain wouldn't make words happen.

"We should stop for now. He's not asleep yet. But Ben, I'll do it. The three weeks."

"The three weeks." He shook his head, trying to get his thoughts back online.

"The trial run. I'll date you for three weeks. I want to try."

"That's good. I want that, too."

"And next time, I don't want to stop so soon."

She was going to kill him. "Whatever you want. We can do that."

Chapter 12

N ell sat at the counter of the flower shop, studying her phone screen. She scanned through the information on the university web page Ben had sent her. She met all the requirements for the scholarship for first-generation college students. The application page said the scholarship was competitive, and not everyone who applied received the funding. But it would cover the full cost of tuition, plus a stipend for books.

If she could find evening classes, and another babysitter, maybe—

She clicked her phone off and shoved it in the back pocket of her jeans. It was too much to plan for right now, but that didn't mean it could never work. Maybe not this year, but next year, when she'd found extra work, saved up some money to pay a sitter.

Ben had challenged himself to do something hard, something that made him uncomfortable. She could do the same. She'd agreed to date him for three weeks, for a start.

Three weeks to get to know him, and not just making conversation. She shivered at the memory of their kiss on the couch last night.

She hadn't imagined the insane chemistry from their first kiss. Feeling like she had to touch him, and if she didn't have more, she'd die. They both wanted more, so why couldn't they have it? Just for a few weeks. Just to see.

She'd felt wanted. Necessary. Even though she didn't believe him when he'd tried to give her credit for his leaving the house, it felt good to be appreciated. Her chest ached at the way he'd looked at her, as if she was good at something, good for him. It would be too easy to want more of that feeling.

It already terrified her, how easily she'd come to trust him. She'd let him into her house, where he should have been out of place with his formal clothes and reserved manners, and instead he'd fit right in. At her dinner table, sitting on the couch with her son.

She couldn't let herself picture a future with him. It was only three weeks, and when the three weeks were up, their relationship would most likely be over, too. Better to have the exit ramp in place. That way, she'd have an easy way out when things didn't go well.

But for now, she would let herself enjoy this time. Three weeks with a gorgeous, stern but gentle man who wanted her, and she wanted him right back.

She grabbed the van keys off the hook and went outside to pull the van around to the front of the shop. They had a large number of deliveries to load today. She backed the van up to the door, parked it, and opened the back doors.

Amy emerged from her office, lifting her chin in greeting. "I'll help you load up today. We'll need to organize things back here to fit it all in."

"I appreciate it."

"Why don't you sit in the back, and I'll hand you the potted plants," Amy said.

Nell nodded and crawled into the van. Amy passed her potted green plants first, which she lined up in rows on the shelves in back. As each plant passed through her hands, she turned it around, checking for dead leaves. She pinched off a couple as she stacked the plants.

When she turned around, Amy's eyes were on her.

"How did you know to do that?" she asked.

"Do what?"

"When you took the leaves off, you pinched the stem in the right place. Above the node."

"Well, that helps it grow better."

"I never told you to do that. Jackie doesn't do it."

Nell gave her a little smile. "I know a few things about plants, I guess from my college classes? But it's also a hobby. I have lots of plants at home."

Amy's brow furrowed. "You've never talked to me about college. You studied botany?"

"Horticulture. But I didn't finish the degree."

"Why didn't you say so on your application? I had no idea."

"Because I didn't finish school. I dropped out. It didn't seem important."

Amy squinted at her in disbelief. "Are you telling me all this time, you knew how to tend these plants like a professional, and you didn't tell me?"

"I just kind of … did it anyway?"

Amy was silent for a moment. She seemed to choose her words carefully before speaking.

"The last few months, some plants have gone missing from the shop, and I couldn't find receipts for them. I thought someone was stealing them." She fixed Nell with a stare.

Nell shook her head, frantic. "Oh, no. I'd never steal them. They didn't like the pots they were in, or the watering schedule, because Jackie always over waters them, so I took them home with me, but I always—"

"You brought them back alive." Amy cracked out a laugh. "The first time one of those damn finicky ferns reappeared looking twice as good as before, I didn't recognize it. I thought someone had left a new plant in the store, which didn't make any sense. Thought I was losing my mind. But it was you, wasn't it? You brought it back after you fixed it up."

Nell crossed her arms over her chest. "It wasn't happy before. Who would have bought it, looking like that?"

"No one, that's who." Amy paused, looking up into the van. "You're a good egg, Nell. But a strange one. There's a lot of stuff you never told me. Next time, no sneaking around. If you want to take a plant home, just tell me. Come on, help me get the bouquets next."

They headed back into the store to collect the wrapped bouquets, which would be stored in buckets on the floor of the van.

"You're not mad at me?" she asked, hefting up a bucket and taking care not to slosh water on her sneakers. She ventured a glance at her boss.

"Not mad. Just surprised. You're overqualified for this job. Why don't you try to finish your degree?"

"Actually, I might. I mean, I'm looking into it. I only have a year's worth of classes left. Well, a year if I went back full time, which I can't. Maybe I could start with one class next year. Or the year after."

"Smart girl like you, you'd breeze through that."

Nell's mouth snapped shut. She'd always thought Amy considered her an idiot.

They walked back to the van together and loaded the bouquets inside.

"It's a matter of finding the time," Nell said. "It's all a big maybe right now."

"Well, don't sit on it too long, if it's what you want."

They finished loading the van in two more trips. Nell crawled out of the van and Amy slammed the door shut. She put her hands on her hips, facing Nell.

"My friend owns a plant nursery in the suburbs. He's looking to hire a couple of managers." She raised a hand to shield her eyes from the sun, squinting at Nell. "I'd tell you to apply, if you had that degree."

"Oh. Well, I'll think about it. For the future." Nell tried not to let disappointment color her voice. Of course a job like that required a degree.

"Or you could apply now, and tell them you'll finish your degree out while you're working there."

Nell stared at her. "They wouldn't hire me."

"Maybe not. I don't know who else applied so far. Not too many people with horticulture degrees." She shrugged. "Up to you. Just thought I'd mention it. I'd give you a recommendation."

Amy turned and went back into the store. Nell stood in the parking lot for a few minutes, holding the keys, but not getting into the driver's seat of the van.

She shook her head and got herself moving. No use getting her hopes up for something that wouldn't happen. Things like that never worked out for her.

"Agnes, it would be a really cool job, though, wouldn't it?" she asked, addressing the chrysanthemum plant riding shotgun in the passenger seat.

She swore the plant nodded at her, or maybe it had just bobbed in the breeze from the open window.

* * *

At 5:00, she was back in her own car, with an over-excited seven year-old bouncing in place in his booster seat.

"How far is it now?" He kicked his feet against the back of the passenger seat.

"About ten more minutes."

"Was he excited when you told him?"

"I'm sure he's very curious to see them."

They'd stopped at the gem shop after she'd picked him up from school, and two of Marco's rocks had crystals inside. He'd demanded they go show them to Ben right away, and Nell had given in and texted him.

"You d-didn't tell him what they look like though, right? That's a surprise."

"No, I didn't tell him."

"Good. Ben said the surprise is the fun part."

She smiled at him in the rearview mirror. "I bet I know what we're doing again this weekend."

"Yeah, we have to go out and look for more. We should ask Ben to come, too. We'd find so many."

"He might not be ready to do that yet. But I know he'd like

to come someday." If Ben was able to go out, and if they had that much time left together.

Ben's door opened as they pulled up to his house. Marco tore off his seatbelt and shot out of the car before Nell could open her own door. She leaned over the roof of the car and watched her normally shy son race up the steps and hold up his geodes for Ben to inspect. His animated chatter carried over the front lawn.

She shut her own door and went to them. Ben knelt down in the doorway, at eye level with Marco. From the breast pocket of his jacket, he extracted a pair of square-framed black reading glasses and slid them on. With his other hand, he held up the geode, inspecting it.

"These are very light, very clear. Definitely quartz. Some-times, they look more cloudy. You did a great job."

"I wanted to find amethyst, but maybe next time."

"The more you look, the more different kinds you'll find. But quartz are the most common." He looked up at Nell and winked.

Her heart turned over in her chest. The glasses were too much, making him somehow several levels hotter. She had the strong urge to pull the glasses off and throw herself at him, but Marco was here, and that wasn't why they'd come. And as far as Marco knew, they were just friends.

"Thanks for letting us drop by. I don't think he could have waited until tomorrow."

Ben straightened to his full height and smiled at her, tucking the glasses back into his pocket. "Of course. It is pretty exciting. Marco, would you like to see my backyard? I have a rock path and a fountain."

"Can we?" Marco looked up at Nell eagerly.

"Sure, but maybe only for a little while. I'm sure Ben is busy."

"Come on in." Ben gestured to them to follow him inside. He led them through the kitchen and out the side door, onto a wooden patio. A pathway lined with rocks circled the yard, leading to a stone fountain by the brick wall at the back. The grass had been cut short, but otherwise, the yard held no other plants.

"Can I go look at the fountain?" Marco asked.

"It's fenced all the way around. It's safe," Ben said.

"Yes, you can go play," she told Marco, and he took off running, following the path to the edge of the yard. Immediately, he plunged his hands into the water streaming from the fountain.

"You have a nice yard. It could use more flowers, though," she said.

"I'm sure it could. I'm not good with plants, like you. But I used to spend more time out here. Before. Do you want to sit?" He gestured at the wrought iron patio chairs.

"It's okay for you? Being outside this long?" She scanned him for signs of anxiety.

"I think so. I've been coming out here a few minutes at a time, mostly at night. Trying to keep my streak going."

"You do have a good streak."

He nodded as they sat together. "Every day this week so far."

Nell couldn't stop herself from reaching over and lacing her fingers with his, greedy to feel his touch again.

"So. I got a babysitter for Saturday. My boss's niece is going to watch Marco. So we can have a real date. No kids."

Ben's gaze snapped to hers. "That sounds good. Would you like to come over here? I can have dinner ready. Or we could try a restaurant ..." His voice turned uncertain.

"Dinner here would be perfect." She squeezed his hand.

"Good. It's a date."

Marco ran across the lawn and gathered a few rocks, then ran back to the fountain to rinse them off in the water.

Ben smiled. "He's so curious about everything."

"He really is. He likes to test out what will happen with everything. Put it in water, break it, throw it."

"A little scientist."

She laughed. "I guess that's true. You're very good with kids. The way you talk to him. You don't have any patients that are children?"

"No. All my patients are adults. But my sister … She was like a kid, and I mean that in the most positive way. Everything was exciting and new. And conversations were straightforward with her. No pretending or hiding things, like adults do. Kids are easier to talk to, really."

"I guess you're right. I'm sorry about your sister. You must miss her so much."

He gave a tight nod. "It's hard to believe we're coming up on the anniversary of her death. My family's Jewish, and one thing I plan to do is mark the date of her passing each year."

"What do Jewish people do on the date?" Nell kept her tone light, but inside she hurt for Ben. His loss was more recent than hers, but the feeling was very familiar.

"Light a candle, say a blessing. And you try to remember them at their best, and … live so you honor their memory."

"What about your parents? Will they be around that day?"

"No. They moved to Arizona after she died. They'd wanted to move for years. I think her death was as hard on them as it was on me, and maybe they also wanted to get away. Start again somewhere else."

"So, you lost your whole family, in a way."

"I guess so. Leah held us together, and then we just … fell apart after." He cleared his throat. "I used to visit her so often. I guess in a way, I felt responsible for her happiness, even as an adult. I was always the one who stuck up for her when we were kids, and I made sure she had what she needed in her community as an adult."

"You were a good big brother."

"I tried to be strong for her. Even when she got sick. And then—" He took a sharp breath and put a hand to his chest. Drew in another short breath.

She rested a hand on his back. His heart raced under her hand. "This is hard for you to talk about. Do you need to go back inside?"

"Yes. I'd better." He stood and opened the patio door, bracing his arm against the handle. "You'll be okay to get Marco?"

"I'll round him up. You go on in."

He gave a quick nod and disappeared inside, probably wanting to pull himself together. She hadn't liked the look on his face a minute ago. Her own grief had been a winding road, full of ups and downs, and Ben's worsened anxiety might be part of the process for him.

She crossed the yard and gathered Marco out of the fountain. The front of his shirt was soaked and streaked with dirt.

"I like Ben's yard. Can we get a fountain too?" he asked.

"Maybe. I'd have to ask permission to put one outdoors at our house. But we need to get going now."

"Did Ben go inside?"

"He did. We'll say goodbye on our way out."

Ben was waiting for them when she slid the patio door open. His breathing was back to normal, and he smiled down at

131

Marco, but the smile looked forced.

"We'll get out of your way," she said. "But please, take care of yourself." She searched his face, looking for signs of anxiety. He seemed put back together, at least on the outside.

"Thank you for coming by," he told Marco, a serious expression on his face. "I'm glad I got to see your geodes."

"And Mom said you'll come with us someday to help us look for more," Marco said.

A pained expression flashed across Ben's face before it closed off again.

"I didn't promise him anything," she said quickly.

Ben gave a clipped nod. "Maybe someday."

Nell ushered Marco to the front door, and Ben followed. He was back to being the reserved, aloof version of himself she'd met that first day. He was protecting himself after almost panicking on the porch, and her heart ached even more. How many times had he braced himself like this, locking down and putting up this armor whenever anxiety hit?

"I'll see you Saturday?" She tried to reach out to him with her eyes, to show him she understood, and it was okay.

"Yes. Saturday." He waved to them and shut the door with a gentle click.

Chapter 13

The next afternoon, Ben sat cross-legged on a crimson velour cushion in The Well Space's relaxation room, trying to focus on his breath. Vanessa had filled the room with soft chairs, colorful lamps, and candles, and patients often used the space as a quiet refuge before or after therapy. He'd never spent much time here.

On a break between patients, he'd come down here—to do what? Try to learn to relax? The room had the opposite of a relaxing effect. The longer he sat here, the more his brain turned to all the things he should be doing upstairs, and also all the ways he'd failed in his progress so far. He'd been at the office for half days, but they needed to be full days. He still wasn't back to normal.

Nell's visit to his house yesterday had made that much painfully clear. He'd gone backwards in his progress during their conversation, and almost had another panic attack. Just when everything seemed like it was back under control, it wasn't. So he'd have to buckle down and try harder, because going back to how he'd been two weeks ago was unacceptable.

Shoulders tense and spine rigid, he gave up and checked his watch. It'd been ten whole minutes—long enough. He unfolded himself from the cushion just as Vanessa walked past the open door. She stopped in her tracks and poked her head inside.

"I don't believe it." A smile played at the corners of her mouth. "Were you meditating?"

"No. I was trying out a breathing exercise."

She raised an eyebrow. "In here?"

"I thought it might be useful. For research purposes. So I'd know what it's like for clients. But I've got an appointment, so I'm heading back up to the office."

Ben never over-explained himself, and Vanessa was onto him in an instant. She arched a brow and blocked his path out the door. Today she wore maroon velvet pants, a pink silk blouse, and her usual sky-high heels.

"Anything else going on?" she asked, scanning him up and down.

He pinched the bridge of his nose. "I don't want to talk about it."

"You never do." She shook her head. "Hey, while you're down here, do you have a minute to stop by my office? I've got some numbers to show you. And maybe I'll get you to spill all your secrets there. Oops, did I say that part out loud?"

"You did. And I won't."

Vanessa excelled at getting secrets out of people. As the senior couples' counselor on staff, she worked with clients through some of the worst relationship problems he'd ever heard of. He was grateful for her expertise in the area—he could never do couples therapy. He just had to stay clear of her prying into his own personal life.

"Come on, Ben. I'll even make you a cup of tea," she offered.

"All right. I've got ten minutes." He shook his head and followed her down the hallway to her office.

Where Ben's office had heavy cherrywood furniture and cream carpeting, Vanessa's office was a riot of pink, red, and floral prints. Along one wall stood a dark pink couch with white and rose-patterned pillows. The windows boasted red silk curtains with beaded ties, and she'd strewn heart-shaped accessories all over the desk.

She boiled water in her kettle, poured it over a tea bag in a mug shaped like cherries, and handed it to him.

"Thank you." He set down the cup on the edge of her desk without drinking. "You've added some new decorations. If Valentine's Day was a room, it would look like this."

A frown creased her brow. "Normally, I'd say good, because that's my favorite holiday. But it's not my favorite anymore. I should re-do this room. Maybe in shades of gray," she huffed as she flopped into her pink desk chair.

"Any particular reason why?"

"My boyfriend broke up with me. I think he was cheating, but I guess I'll never find out for sure." She stirred her own tea too vigorously with the tiny silver spoon.

"Oh. I'm sorry to hear it."

"Well, it's better I find out now, rather than later, that he's a cheating cheater who cheats."

"Definitely. But I remember you saying this guy was special. You were sure he was the one."

"Well, he wasn't."

"I'm sorry," Ben repeated. It was a really good thing he wasn't a couples counselor.

"Well. Enough about my love life. Let's talk about your problems."

"You said you had some numbers to go over?"

She rolled her eyes at him. "Fine. Yes, let me pull up the report."

Ben sat across from her and she turned her computer screen so he could see the numbers.

"Overall, appointment numbers are down from last year. Fewer new patients are coming into the practice, but also, we had a few leave, like I told you."

"Have we seen any change in that trend in the last two weeks?"

"Since the flowers you sent and the social media posts we were tagged in, we haven't had any more patients leave. So that's the good news."

"And the bad news is …"

Vanessa cradled her cup in her hands, blowing steam across the top of it. "The bad news is, we need to get some of those patients to return, or else book new patients who might still be deciding which provider they want to use. We've stopped the exodus, but we need to see an increase again."

Ben rubbed a hand over his forehead. "I've been brainstorming ideas on that front. I've outlined a patient referral program I think could bring in new people. I'll email it to you once I'm back at my desk."

"That sounds great. I'm not sure why we haven't had a referral program in place before."

"We didn't need one before. We had more patients than we could handle for a while there. But since I …"

"You haven't been around as much," she supplied.

"Right. Since that. I haven't gone to any conferences, or

done any book signings or local events, like I used to. I know I need to be back full time. I'm still planning to go to Chicago to accept the award. I'm going to think of a way to fix this."

He couldn't lose the clinic, the goal he'd worked toward for the last decade.

"I might be able to help you fix it if I knew what was going on," she said softly.

Ben met her steady green gaze, and suddenly didn't feel like lying anymore. He jumped from his seat and paced the length of her office.

"I'm going to tell you what's going on, but you will not tell anyone else at the clinic. This stays between you and me."

Vanessa set down her cup, her expression turning serious. "Of course. I'd never break your confidence."

"I know. That's why I'm telling you." He took a deep breath. "The reason I haven't been here is because I seem to have … It's gotten worse over the last year, but I've always …"

He dropped back into his chair and made himself say it. "I have generalized anxiety disorder. With agoraphobia. And panic attacks." There. It was out in the open. Unlike him. "I've always had it, but this year it's gotten worse. I haven't been able to control it as well as I could before."

"You've … always had it?" Her brow creased in a tiny frown.

"Yes. But I take medication, and it was always under control. Until recently. Some days, I couldn't even …" He cleared his throat. "I couldn't go out and get the mail."

Vanessa's eyes fixed on him, wide with shock and sadness. "Why didn't you tell me? Did you think I wouldn't understand?"

"It's not that. It's that people counted on me to be in charge. I had so much to take care of, and if people knew, they'd think I needed help. That I couldn't manage everything, when I can.

I'll get past this episode and things will be back to normal, I promise."

She leaned back in her chair, silent for a long moment before speaking. "I am so, so angry at you right now."

"I'm sorry. I know I should have told you earlier."

"Not because you didn't tell me, you idiot. Because you didn't get help for yourself. God, Ben, did you not think you deserved to be helped, same as any of your patients?"

"I didn't think of it that way. With everything I know, I thought I should be able to take care of it on my own. And I kept it in check just fine, for years. Until I couldn't. But I've adjusted my meds now, and I'm getting better. I'm here, right?"

She let out a breath. "Yes. You are. And we're glad to have you back. But don't push yourself. Now that I know what's happening, we can plan better. We'll be careful with your schedule so we don't overload you with patients. We'll schedule local events with someone else. We can work around this."

"But that's exactly what I don't want. I don't want accommodations. I don't want people looking at me like something's wrong with me. Feeling sorry for me."

"That's not what this is—"

"No one finds out what's going on." He stood and folded his arms over his chest, tone steely.

"Of course not. I only want to help you. We're friends first, not just coworkers. You know that."

Vanessa rose from her chair and approached him. She opened her arms and folded him into an awkward hug, which he tried to return, but his spine remained stiff with tension.

They broke apart, and he cleared his throat. "I'm headed back upstairs. I have a client in twenty."

"Thank you for telling me," she said. "I can't imagine how

hard this past month has been for you. I wish you had family here, someone to help you out."

"Well." He cleared his throat. "There is someone who's helped me. Helped me a lot more than the medication, if I'm honest. We're dating."

Where this sudden urge to tell Vanessa about his personal life had come from, he didn't know. Maybe it was the atmosphere in her pink and red office, all plastered in hearts.

Her eyes lit up. "Ooh, this is better than Valentine's Day. Tell me about her."

"She's a single mom. She accidentally delivered flowers to my house, and I had a panic attack right in front of her. That's how we met. The least romantic meeting of all time."

"Hmm." Vanessa folded her arms over her chest, considering him.

"She's different from anyone I've known. I want things to work out with her. But I don't know if I'm strong enough."

She frowned. "What do you mean?"

"Yesterday, I almost had another panic attack, sitting with her on my patio. She's had a hard time in the past, and she deserves someone who can take care of her, but how can I do that if I'm not well? What if I never get better, or I get better and then it happens again?"

"Ben. Would you tell any of your patients they can't be in a relationship, just because they have anxiety?"

"Of course not."

"You know what's wrong. You're taking steps to get better. In fact, it seems like she's the difference."

"She is. She makes me want to get better."

"I wish you could see your face when you talk about her. So soft, when you're normally all closed off. Sorry. No offense."

"None taken."

Vanessa tapped a finger on her chin. "I'm having a theory."

"Oh, no."

"No, hear me out a minute. You're normally all closed off because you like to be in control of everything. But from the very start, you let yourself drop your control around her. Or you had to, in a way. Your anxiety forced you to do that. She's seen you not be in control, not be in charge of everything for once. And maybe that's what you needed. To have to show your real self to another person."

"I—" Ben snapped his mouth shut. Vanessa was far, far too good at her job. "You could be right about that. Possibly."

She patted his arm. "I'm always right about love." Then she frowned. "Except my own love life. There, I couldn't tell you what went wrong."

* * *

That night after work, Ben put on his running clothes—athletic shorts and a thermal long-sleeve top. The spring air would still be chilly in the evening this time of year. He laced up his running shoes, the same brand he'd worn for years. This particular pair had no dirt from outside on the soles.

He would put on the same clothes to run on his treadmill, but that wasn't his plan tonight. He was going outside. The itchy feeling was back under his skin, like he needed to move, to get fresh air. He'd been trapped in the cage of his house for too long.

At the front door, he didn't let himself hesitate. He grabbed his keys, stepped out the door, and shut it behind him. On the porch, he did a couple of warm-up stretches, careful to keep his gaze down. The less he looked around, the better.

One sprint around the block would take three and a half minutes, if his treadmill times were comparable to an outdoor run. In three and a half minutes, how much could go wrong? He'd sat on the patio for longer than that at this point.

Eyes down, deep breaths. He ran down his steps to the sidewalk, then eased into a jog. His sneakers ate up the pavement, thudding to the time of his heartbeat. Time to open up into a run.

Drawing his elbows tight to his sides, Ben lengthened his strides into a sprint. His long legs ate up the distance and soon he'd reached the first turn of the block. A woman pushing a stroller appeared in his peripheral vision, but in front of him, it was just pavement and his own feet.

His breath echoed in his ears, accelerated from running, but not a panic attack. Another minute and he'd be around the second corner.

He increased his pace a notch, coming close to his top speed. And there it was—the moment when his breath and heartbeat and the straining of his muscles all fell away, and there were no thoughts, no anxiety, only pure exertion. Heaven. This was why he ran, why he would always be a runner.

He rounded the final corner on the block and slowed a fraction as he approached his porch. He took the steps two at a time, and jogged in place for a few minutes to cool down. He rested his hands on his knees, breath going fast, sweat dripping down the sides of his face and soaking his shirt.

An unexpected laugh bubbled out of him. His first run outdoors in over a month. Tomorrow, he'd go again, for longer.

He'd always told his patients there would be bad days and good days in the fight. And this was one of the good ones.

Chapter 14

Nell was fifteen minutes late when she rang Ben's doorbell on Saturday night, and not just because she'd spent a lot longer than usual getting ready. After a long debate, she'd settled on a mid-thigh length sundress with a halter neck and a black and daisy print, paired with her white sneakers. Ben would be more dressed up than she was, but there was no way to avoid that. The man always looked like he'd just stepped out of a clothing ad.

But now that she knew what he looked like with his hair rumpled and his shirt unbuttoned ... She shivered. Messing him up again could be fun.

Marco had been thrilled with his new babysitter, Amy's niece, who'd brought books and craft supplies along with her. He'd barely waved goodbye as they settled into a slime-making project in the kitchen.

She couldn't blame her lateness on Marco, or anything else other than nerves. Ben had been so reserved the last time she'd seen him, the afternoon they'd sat on his patio, and she hadn't seen him since. When he opened the door, she wasn't sure which version of Ben she'd find—the aloof, formal one, or the one with the soft, kind eyes. The one who'd told her she was beautiful, a memory she'd relived more than once this week.

"Only one way to find out," she told herself as she checked her makeup one last time in the rearview mirror and climbed out of her car.

Ben opened the door and stared at her for a long minute, long enough that she suddenly doubted everything. This would be worse than awkward, worse than their first meeting.

"You said 6:00, right? I'm sorry I'm a few minutes late."

Ben cleared his throat. "Yes. Sorry. Come on in." He stepped back and she followed him inside. He shut the door behind them and turned to face her. Another long moment of silence.

"Your, uh … Your hair is down." Ben gestured in the direction of her head.

"Oh. Yeah, I leave it down once in a while." She'd clipped the long waves to one side with a barrette, and the length of it fell down to her mid-back. Impractical hair, most days.

"It's so long. I didn't realize." His eyes continued roaming over her, and warmth flooded her face.

"I like it," he said, his voice sounding deeper than usual.

"Thank you. You look nice, too." He wore charcoal dress pants and a black button-down. No vest, tie, or jacket tonight, which was his version of casual. He looked sharp and luxurious, and also nervous.

He opened his mouth as if about to say something else, then shut it.

"I can get you a glass of wine, if you want?" he asked after a beat.

"Sure."

The word unfroze him, and he went to the counter, where he'd uncorked a bottle of merlot, and poured her a glass. She cradled the glass in the palm of her hand, took a sip, then set it down.

"Is something wrong? We can do this another time, if you're not feeling—"

"Nothing's wrong." He shook his head, shutting his eyes for a moment. "God, I'm sorry. I made all these plans for tonight, and it's awkward already, isn't it?"

"The last time I saw you, we had a hard conversation. You seemed like you wanted your privacy afterward. And to be honest, part of me thought you wouldn't even want to go ahead with this date."

"That's not it." He set down his glass and braced a hand on the counter. "I do want to do this. But I think … I'm still struggling with the contrast between what I could do before, and what I can do now. I had a nice dinner delivered by caterers. I set up the dining table with actual china and cloth napkins. When I planned all this, I thought it would be as good as a restaurant, as good as taking you out on a real date. But the truth is, I feel ridiculous. If I'd met you a year ago, I would have taken you out someplace nice. This is not good enough for you. I mean, look at you."

"What about me?" She took a step closer to him.

"You're so beautiful, it hurts my eyes. And I'm—"

"Ben," she interrupted.

He took a shaky breath. "What."

"Would you please kiss me hello?"

He stared at her for a moment, then his arm snagged around her waist, pulling her close. His mouth came down on hers, and in an instant, the connection was back, the feeling of rightness

145

and safety. She looped her arms around his neck and poured that feeling into the kiss.

She eased her mouth away from him a minute later, keeping their faces a few inches apart.

"I feel better now. How about you?" she asked.

"Yes. Better."

She stroked a hand down the side of his face, brushing over the smooth waves at his temple.

"I don't want a restaurant or a fancy night out. I want to enjoy our time together. I'm happy when I'm with you."

"Me too," he said, his voice rough around the edges.

"Then let's be happy." She laced her fingers with his. "Come on, show me this gourmet dinner you had delivered."

He had silver chafing dishes set up in the dining room, keeping the food hot. He'd arranged white china place settings on opposite sides of the square table. A pair of long tapered candles and a bouquet of roses completed the romantic setup.

"This is beautiful," she said. "But there's one problem."

"What's wrong?" Ben scanned the table as if something offensive might be lurking underneath it.

"I don't want to sit across from you. Can we move my place so I'm sitting next to you?"

"Of course."

They moved the place settings, and Ben uncovered the dishes to reveal braised short ribs and stuffed chicken, mashed potatoes and roasted vegetables. A mixed fruit tart and a basket of bread sat in the center of the table, along with a pitcher of ice water and another bottle of wine, a chilled white.

"You thought of everything," she said.

"I wasn't sure what you liked. I hope this is close."

"This is the nicest meal I've had in a long time, and I haven't even tried it yet."

Seated at the table, Nell hooked her ankle around Ben's and ran a foot up the side of his calf. His eyes jerked up to meet hers and she gave him a wide smile. He was so reserved, it was fun to play around with him, to do things that shocked him a little bit.

They started eating, and he relaxed, telling her about his past few days at the clinic, and his recent outdoor running adventures. She told him about Amy finding out she'd been taking plants home to doctor them up, and he threw back his head and laughed.

He always listened to her so carefully, his dark eyes never leaving her face, which was probably why she found herself telling him about the job opportunity with Amy's friend.

"I'm not qualified, but Amy said she'd give me a recommen- dation letter."

"You should apply. You never know if they'd call you in for an interview."

She chewed on her lip. "Maybe. But maybe it's just one more thing I wouldn't get, you know?"

"I know you've had a lot of disappointments. It takes courage to keep trying, after all that."

"I might do it. I'm not sure." She cleared her throat, eager for a subject change. "So. It's the end of week one. Of the three-week period."

"It is."

"Do you want to keep going for week two?"

His expression turned serious. "You know I do. If you can put up with me for another week."

"I think I can manage it, after this amazing dinner." She patted her stomach. "I can't do dessert yet."

"Do you want to see my patio at night? It's got lights. We could sit out there."

"That would be okay with you?"

"Yes, for a while. The dark is easier to deal with than daylight."

She grinned at him. "I knew you were part vampire."

Ben led her to the patio door, and a gasp of surprise escaped her when he opened it.

"It's like a fairy garden." Strings of tiny white lights lined the patio, the rock path illuminated by sconces on either side. Submerged lamps lit the fountain on the back wall too, the water falling in bright streams down the rocks.

"I thought you'd like it. You like fairy gardens, if I remember right."

Her eyes flew to his. "I do. I always imagined how I'd landscape my own someday. Of course, I live in a rental house, so I can't do that yet. But one day …"

Ben's hand was warm on the small of her back, guiding her to the patio bench. They sat together, looking out over the darkened yard. Out here, time stood still, with no worries about money or parenting to deal with.

Contentment warmed her from the inside, and on impulse, she leaned and put her head on Ben's shoulder. So what if this was all only temporary. It felt good, and she would let herself have more of that feeling.

Ben turned his face toward her, his dark eyes glinting in the glow from the fairy lights. "Do you want to walk down the path? See the fountain?"

She nodded, the movement in slow motion, dreamy. "Let's go."

He took her hand and led her down the curving path through

the center of the yard. The path lights caught on the crystal flecks in the rocks, making them glitter. The hum of running water increased as they approached the high brick wall at the back of the yard, where the fountain overflowed, cascading down three tiers of stones.

Nell reached out a hand, trailing her fingers through the falling water. "I love it. It's so peaceful."

"I've come out here the past few evenings. But it's better with you here." Ben's voice was low and close to her ear. He wrapped his arms around her waist, hugging her from behind.

He was so solid, and she let herself lean back into him. The crisp cotton of his dress shirt pressed against the bare skin of her upper back. She was achingly conscious of the man beneath, strong and warm.

His mouth brushed over the bare skin at the base of her neck and she shivered, tilting her head to the side to give him more access. His arms tightened around her waist, mouth moving up her neck to the spot under her ear. He inhaled there, then placed an open-mouthed kiss on the spot.

Her breath left her on a puff and her knees went weak, just like they'd done the first time he'd kissed her. She had no choice but to lean into him, and he held her up easily. One arm stayed wrapped around her middle, but his other hand trailed upward, coming to rest on the tie at the neck of her sundress.

"Can I open this?" His voice was sandpaper rough. His fingers hesitated on the edge of the fabric, toying with the string. "I've been dying to touch you. It's all I thought about this week."

"Yes." She'd die if he stopped. Her heart thundered close to his fingers, rushing in her ears.

He tugged the knot open and let the top half of the dress

drop, baring her breasts as the fabric fell away.

A rough sound came out of him. "So beautiful."

His hands stroked over her, soft and light, his thumbs grazing over her nipples. Her breath accelerated, skin pebbling into goosebumps.

"Ever since I opened the door tonight, all I could think about was doing this." His voice was a deep rumble in her ear. "Your hair. This dress. It's too much. I couldn't think, looking at you."

He nipped her earlobe between his teeth and another gasp escaped her. A vicious throb built at her center. It had been fun to tease him at dinner, shock him out of his usual reserve, but now, with him touching her like this, she was in way over her head. She pushed against his hands, needing more, needing something.

She turned her head sideways, and his mouth was right there, meeting hers in a messy kiss. Not careful or gentle. She threaded her fingers into his sleek, soft hair and arched back into him. His hot arousal pressed against her lower back, and she wanted it, whatever they could have, as much as he'd give her.

He would take good care of her. She could let herself have this.

She pulled her mouth away from his, out of breath. "Ben. Take me inside."

His eyes glittered down at her. "And what will I do with you inside?"

She turned in his arms, facing him. "Have me. If you want me."

He set his jaw, grabbed her hand, and led her back up the path toward the house. She didn't bother to retie the neck of her dress, and the cool night air stirred against her bare torso, transforming her into a fairy, another creature of the garden at night.

Once they were inside, Ben went straight up the staircase, still holding her hand. He led her down the hallway to his bedroom, where a king-size bed with a heavy oak frame dominated the space, piled high with navy and cream bedding.

He flicked on the bedside lamp and sat on the end of the bed, pulling her so she stood between his knees. He shoved a hand through his hair, gaze hot as it raked over her form, naked to the waist.

"I could look at you all day." His voice was mostly gravel. "I'm halfway convinced you'll disappear as soon as I touch you again. Maybe I'm imagining this."

She brushed a thumb over his mouth, loving the way his breath hitched in response.

"You're not imagining it. Please, touch me again."

He swallowed. "Birth control?"

"I haven't been with anyone in six years, and I've been tested. And I can't get pregnant. So we don't have to use a condom, if you don't want to."

His eyes darkened. "It's been a while for me, too. And I was tested a year ago."

"Good." She crushed her mouth down on his. His hands came up to her waist, tugging at the dress until it dropped to the floor. She stepped out of it, now wearing only her tiniest pair of black silk underwear.

His mouth roamed over her stomach, pressing kisses in a line from one hipbone to the other. He palmed her hips, pulling her closer. The movement pulled her off balance, and she braced her arms on his shoulders.

He gave another tug, pulling her down onto his lap until she straddled him, and she kissed him some more, urgency taking over her body.

She worked open the buttons of his shirt with frantic fingers, not recognizing herself. In the past, sex had been a series of motions to go through to please her partner, and she could follow the routine almost without paying attention. But this was different. She was fully present, and she needed more, and now.

She tried to push his shirt off, but the fabric got stuck on his wrists at the cuffs, and she abandoned the garment, her hands too eager to explore. His torso was hot and smooth, leanly muscled, broad at the shoulders, and dusted with lots of dark hair that narrowed to a trail at his waist. The muscles under her palms jumped at her touch. He watched her touching him for a moment, his chest heaving, before stopping her with a hand on her wrist.

"Wait." He drew back and eased her off his lap, onto the bed, and she leaned back on her elbows, watching him. He stood and peeled his shirt the rest of the way off with unsteady hands. His fingers stilled when they got to the button of his pants. He stared down at her for a long moment, eyes glittering hot.

"I wish you could see yourself." He discarded his pants and stood facing her in his black boxer briefs, which strained with an impressive erection. "You're amazing."

"Come here." She held out an arm to him and he lowered himself onto the bed beside her. His face was inches from hers, and he reached up a hand to cup the side of her face. The look in his eyes held enough tenderness to drown in. She was dying for him to kiss her again, but he didn't.

"Tell me what you like. So I can give it to you." His whispered words made her shiver.

No one had ever asked her that, and no answer came to mind. She liked everything they'd done so far, and that was as much as she knew.

"I don't know. But don't stop." She made a little sound of frustration as she reached for him.

"Hmm. Let's see if we can figure it out." He bypassed her mouth and went back to kissing her neck and stroking her breasts, his torso still resting between her legs. When she was squirming and pushing up against him, wordlessly begging for more, his hand slid to the apex of her thighs, rubbing her through the silk, back and forth.

His touch was gentle, exploring at first. He followed her responses, figuring out what made her gasp and shiver. Then his fingers grew more confident, touching her in a way that felt exactly right and brand new at the same time, until her fingers curled into his shoulders and tension coiled inside her, unbearably tight and hot.

Ben didn't let her mentally check out. He kept her with him, taking her apart piece by piece, pulling more and deeper sensations out of her. She was dissolving from the inside out, and she needed more, just the smallest push to go over the edge.

His fingers slid under the silk and stroked her once, twice with perfect pressure. Her body arched back, and the first wave of pleasure detonated. It went on and on, leaving her wrecked. She stared up at him, flushed and dazed.

"That's one thing you like." He lowered his mouth to hers for a lazy, soft kiss. Beneath the gentleness of his mouth, she could feel the tension in him, the fine shaking in the muscles of his shoulders. After a minute, he was breathing harder, kissing her with more urgency.

She reached down and slid her underwear down her legs, and he tracked the movement hotly. He stood and pushed down his boxer briefs, and she only had a moment to admire his naked form before he was back over her, sliding a hand under her hips to tilt her up for him.

"Tell me if it's too much. Or if you want to stop. But I have to—"

He pushed inside her in a slow movement. His eyes slammed shut and he held himself still for a minute above her, bracing his free hand on the bed. He shifted back, a small movement, then pushed in deeper.

"All right?" he ground out.

"Yes. I'm good. It's good." The intense feeling of fullness, the heat of his skin against her, all of it was good.

"God, Nell." He tested a couple of movements, frowning in concentration as he tried one angle, then another, until he found one that forced a startled cry of pleasure from her.

"There." Satisfaction laced his voice and he started to move in earnest, each stroke building up the hot pressure again inside her.

Her hands roamed up his sides and back, feeling the muscles bunch and shift. She'd cracked open, and all her empty spaces were filled with him, his heat and breath and closeness.

She'd given herself a chance to feel something again, and it was worth it. He was worth falling apart for. A broken moan escaped as the tension shattered her from the inside, and she yanked his torso closer, trying to get him deeper inside her where he'd never leave.

He groaned and came with her, abdomen tensing, arms rigid on either side of her body. As his breathing slowed, his hand came up to cup the side of her face. The gesture was becoming a habit.

"That was …"

"It was perfect," she told him, even though the word wasn't right, or enough.

"Good." He dropped his head into her neck and inhaled. "It was … perfect for me, too. Give me thirty minutes, and I'll find out what else you like."

He rolled to his side and pulled her in close to his chest, wrapping an arm around her back as she tucked her head under his chin. He was silent for a few minutes, his hand rubbing up and down her back. She placed her hand in the center of his chest, feeling the slowing heartbeat there, contentment warming her from the inside.

"I'm glad I dropped those flowers on your porch," she said a minute later, already drifting off. He'd keep her safe while she slept, and then he'd wake her for more.

A soft laugh huffed out of him. "Not as glad as I am."

Chapter 15

Nell smiled and chatted with all the plants as she loaded the day's deliveries into the back of the van. She'd smiled a lot the past few days—real smiles, not fake ones. She couldn't share the reason why with Amy, and definitely not with Marco, but a secret happiness had bloomed in her chest. He was hers, for two more weeks at least.

A lot could happen in two weeks. It would be smarter not to let her heart get too involved yet. And above all, she had to keep Marco out of this. He couldn't know she was dating Ben.

But still, she had two weeks. She wouldn't think beyond that, because the future never worked out the way you planned, anyway. She'd enjoy her time with Ben now, while everything felt magical and new. She couldn't stop herself smiling again, picturing his backyard at night, the fairy lights, and the way he'd made her feel.

It had been two days since she'd seen him, and she missed him more than she'd have thought possible.

She'd gone home that night and paid the babysitter in a haze of happiness. Marco had already been asleep, and Nell had slipped into bed, still feeling the sensation of Ben's arms around her and smelling his cologne on her skin.

The next morning, she'd applied for the college scholarship. She sat at her laptop for almost two hours, filling out the online form. It had been surprisingly detailed, with multiple questions about her parents and upbringing.

She'd never known her dad. Mom had worked two jobs, one at a dry cleaners, and the other cleaning houses for wealthy folks in her off hours. Nell's life wasn't so different now, scrambling to make ends meet.

Mom should have gotten to meet her grandson. And she'd be proud of Nell, trying to finish college now. Filling out this application was the right choice, even though she wasn't sure how she'd manage her work schedule and classes, if she did get the scholarship.

She also applied for a dozen more part-time jobs while she was at it, still looking for a third job to boost her income. At the last minute, she filled out the job application for the manager position at the plant nursery with Amy's friend. It was a long shot, but what was one more application added to the pile?

Maybe she was good enough for a better job. Maybe she just hadn't let herself try, or hadn't felt like she stood a chance. But she was trying all kinds of things she'd never let herself imagine in the last six years.

At lunchtime, Ben texted her.

Do you want to go for a run after work?

I'm not in as good shape as you are. But if you go slow, sure.

You do realize this run will only be five to seven minutes long.

She smiled down at her phone.

> *Well, I can manage five minutes.*

Maybe I should keep all my runs to five minutes. So you can always come along.

> *Someday soon, you'll be running miles.*

She clicked the phone off. She wouldn't tell Ben about applying for the scholarship and the manager job. Both applications would likely end in rejections, and this way, she wouldn't have to share the bad news with him later. If good news came, she'd tell him.

When she pulled up to his house, he was already waiting on the porch. A ridiculous surge of happiness exploded in her chest at the sight of him.

She scanned his lean frame as she approached, not bothering to hide the fact that she was staring.

"You're wearing shorts," she said. The black nylon running shorts hit him at mid-thigh, showing off legs that were toned, heavy with muscle.

"It's seventy-five degrees."

"I've never seen you in workout clothes. This might be a problem."

He frowned in confusion. "A problem?"

"Mmm." She stepped closer and wrapped her arms around him. "You look very nice in your running gear." Her hands ran up his back, exploring the muscles beneath the thin T-shirt.

His gaze darkened, pupils dilating. "Don't get me started. I haven't thought of much else in the last few days."

"Me neither," she admitted.

"And we don't have time for anything else right now, so you should absolutely stop looking at me like that. Stop." A dull red flush stained his cheeks.

"I can't help it. You're too attractive."

He made a frustrated sound and planted a firm kiss on her mouth before stepping away.

"We're going running now. Nothing else," he said, as if convincing himself.

"Running." She took a deep breath. "All right, let's go."

They took off at a moderate jog around his block. She'd worn track pants and sneakers to work, so she was able to keep up with him, but he was obviously going slower for her sake. If he took off sprinting, she'd never catch him.

As they rounded the first corner of his block, he held up a hand. "Wait a second."

He jogged off the sidewalk, down into a small drainage ditch by the side of the road. A minute later, he was back, holding up a rock.

"It's a quartz. You can give it to Marco for his collection."

"Of course." She swallowed, pocketing the crystal. "He'll love it."

He resumed his jog. "We should get him a display case."

Nell groaned. "Oh my God, I'm not sure I want him to know a display case is a possibility."

He flashed her a grin. "Welcome to having a rock collector in the family."

When they got back to Ben's house, he wasn't even winded.

"I guess that was pretty easy for you," she said, bracing her hands on her knees.

"Physically, yes." He cut his gaze away from her to the side.

"Oh. For a minute, I almost forgot about—"

"It's fine. I increased my time by two minutes. So I call it a win."

"I agree." She cleared her throat. "So, not to change the subject. But if you want to come over again sometime. Maybe after Marco goes to bed? He takes a while to fall asleep, but then he sleeps like the dead."

"Does he." The hot gleam returned to Ben's eyes.

"Yes. He doesn't, um, wake up very easily once he's out."

"I'll be over tonight. If that works for you."

He sent her back to her car with another too-brief kiss and a soft pat on her hip, which she somehow managed to feel throughout her whole body.

* * *

At 8:30 that night, a quiet knock had her jumping up off the couch and running to open the door. She flung herself into Ben's arms, kissing him mindlessly as they stumbled inside. She kicked the door shut with her foot and sank deeper into his embrace. Nothing could touch this feeling, that when he was close, everything was right.

Upstairs, behind her locked door, she pressed a forearm over her mouth to muffle her cries as he made love to her, bringing her over the edge again and again. He touched her a hundred different ways, pulling out more responses she hadn't known lived inside her. And she got braver, exploring his body, tasting and touching while he watched her with glittering eyes.

Afterward, she curled on her side and he spooned her from behind. His arm wrapped securely around her middle and his face rested in the hollow of her neck. He placed a gentle kiss there, then one on her ear, then her temple.

She shivered and relaxed further into him, absorbing his warmth.

"Talk to me so I stay awake," she told him after her third yawn. "I want to be with you a little longer."

"What should I talk about? How beautiful you are?" Ben's voice was sleepy, satisfied and relaxed in a way no one got to hear but her.

She ducked her head. "Not that."

"But it's a good subject. For example, have you seen your eyes?"

"Stop."

"They're extraordinary. They contain at least five different shades of gray and blue."

She turned her head to look at him over her shoulder. "They do not."

"They do. I've studied them a lot. I couldn't stop looking at them, since the first day we met. I looked down at you, kneeling on my porch in the broken glass, and my thoughts stopped. Your eyes have an effect on me. They hypnotize me. I can't resist them." His hands roamed down her body again, with increasing purpose.

"Ben. That's ridiculous." She shut her eyes and looked away, embarrassed and turned on despite herself.

"And then there's your hair. Did you know, I could smell your shampoo every time we were in the van together? It drove me crazy. Hundreds of flowers in that van with us, and all I could smell was you."

"Please … Let's talk about something else."

He turned her face toward him again with a finger on her chin. "Why?"

With his face this close, she had nowhere to hide. "Because I don't like compliments."

"You don't believe them. Right?"

"I guess so."

"Well, this is my perception. You can't argue with my perception. And maybe you don't believe it, but I do."

"Okay," she whispered. Ben believed a lot of things about her that might not be true. But maybe it wasn't so bad, having someone see the good in you.

He squeezed her gently, settling her back into his arms. "Good. And … you probably don't want me to spend the night?"

She tensed in his arms. "I can't. Not yet. Marco will wake up in the morning, and—"

"I understand. It's too soon."

"Exactly. I don't want him thinking we're dating. It would be too hard for him if it doesn't work out."

A long pause. "I'm hoping for a more positive outcome."

She hugged his arm. A part of her—a big part—wanted that positive outcome, too. But wanting things didn't mean they'd happen.

"It's too early to know, though. That's why we're trying it out, right?" She kept her voice as light as possible.

"You're right. Of course." His arm tightened around her.

After a few minutes, she drifted, growing more relaxed in his embrace. It would be so nice to curl up and sleep, wrapped up like this.

"Did you know, falling asleep was the hardest part for me,

after I got divorced?" she asked after another yawn.

"Why was that?"

"I think I felt unsafe. All alone in the house with a two year-old. I'd lie there thinking I heard noises, imagining the worst. Sometimes I went and slept on the floor in Marco's room."

"I'm sorry. I wish I could have been there." His hand stroked over her hair, as if he couldn't help touching it some more.

"I got used to it. I'm glad you're here, though." Her eyes drifted shut again.

She was jostled awake by Ben climbing out of the bed. A glance at her phone told her it was after 11:00. She sat up in a rush, pulling a T-shirt over her head.

"I can let myself out. I didn't want to wake you up," he said.

"It's fine. I have to lock up anyway." She followed him downstairs, enjoying all over again the sight of his broad shoulders and tousled hair. He looked better, a little bit messed up.

At her front door, he kissed her softly. "I hope you have good dreams."

"You too."

"And I'll see you soon. Maybe tomorrow?"

"Same time, same place."

Chapter 16

Ben walked Penny to the door of his office, after they'd finished their first in-person therapy session in a month. She was all relaxed smiles today, a stark contrast to the last time he'd seen her, the day he'd sent her to the emergency room.

"I want to apologize again, for coming here in the state I was in." She shook her head, shifting her blonde bob from side to side. "In my right mind, I never would have done that."

"No apologies needed. You coming in that day gave me a good reminder to contact all the physicians of my patients about their medications. I can't assume their doctors will check the records from other providers. So you did me a service."

"I don't know about that. I'm still pretty embarrassed."

"It will prevent what happened to you from happening to anyone else."

"I guess you're right." She fiddled with the clasp on her purse, lingering in the doorway.

"It's not embarrassing to ask for help, or to need help."

He should take his own advice. Vanessa would have a field day if she'd heard him say that last sentence.

"I want to thank you for the flowers you sent a couple of weeks ago, too. It was such a nice gesture," she said.

"Of course. Flowers are good for mental health."

"Oh, they are. You can't be sad around flowers. And I saw on social media that you'd sent flowers to some of your other patients, too."

"That's right. We sent out quite a few."

Her brow furrowed. "Did you send them to everyone, then? That must have been expensive."

Ben froze, then forced his shoulders to relax. Clearly, she wanted an explanation. "Yes, we sent them to everyone. We wanted to show how much we appreciate all our patients."

"You know, I was talking to my friend Beverly. She's a patient of yours, too? She was worried she hadn't seen you in person for a while. She said she'd called and asked for an appointment, but the only ones available were video calls. But I told her I'd seen you twice in two weeks, so there was nothing to worry about."

Penny leaned forward, as if sharing a secret. "Anyway, Beverly heard some people were leaving the clinic. I told her not to pay attention to gossip. Who'd want to leave this place? You all are the best."

"Thank you. That means a lot. And we'll be here for a long time to come."

"I'm glad. And I got the email about your referral program. I'll definitely tell my friends. In case you need more patients, which I'm sure you don't."

"We'd appreciate it."

He waved goodbye to her and shut the door, then sank down

into his desk chair, rubbing a hand over his forehead.

If Penny had made the connection that other people hadn't seen him in person, how many other patients had, too? He had to be here, to be reliable and available. Maybe if Nell was in his life long-term, he could take on working at the clinic full-time again.

He opened his office door and went to Cameron's desk in the waiting room. His assistant stabbed at his salad with a fork while he squinted through his glasses at a spreadsheet on his computer screen. He had earbuds in his ears, and didn't notice Ben approaching.

"Cameron."

The younger man jumped and pulled out his earbud. "Sorry. Yes. Did you need something?"

"When people have been calling to make appointments, and you give them the option of an in-person appointment, what have their responses been?"

"Oh, um. Mostly good." He shifted around in his chair, looking uncomfortable. His suspenders of the day had a galaxy of stars, along with tiny starships.

"Some people were surprised, but they were happy to have the choice. Others still want to keep their video calls."

"And they didn't say anything negative? No one was impatient with you?"

"Well. One woman said, 'About damn time.' And another one said she'd been thinking of switching doctors. But it's mostly been positive."

"That's good. Will you let me know if anyone gives you trouble about it?"

"Of course."

Ben frowned. "And Cameron. You can eat lunch away from

your desk. Maybe take a walk on your break?"

"I know I can." The younger man shrugged. "I get more done this way. Grad school is kicking my ass."

"I remember that well."

Cameron bobbed his head, put his earbud back in, and returned to studying his screen.

Ben kept frowning as he went back into his office and shut the door behind him. Was no one in this entire clinic practicing what they preached? The Well Space was dedicated to helping people find good mental health, in theory.

In practice, they had employees working through their lunch breaks, arriving before 7:00 a.m. Suffering from anxiety and panic attacks, in his own case. And in Vanessa's case, chronic relationship problems, even though she was an expert on love. She'd broken up with a dozen men since he'd known her.

He sank into his desk chair again. He'd had a giant blind spot when it came to his own clinic, his baby, and that was unacceptable. Everyone deserved to experience the kind of happiness he'd only started to discover the last two weeks.

He spent the afternoon in his office, making it his first full day outside his house. Vanessa's patient intake reports for the week were reassuring. The referral program had brought in a few new people. He'd been able to stay at the clinic for longer periods of time, and he didn't feel as tired as he had during his first week back.

Everything was better, including the inside of him. He hadn't had a panic attack in over a week. Maybe he'd defeated the anxiety again, pushed it back into the dark where it belonged. He could have his life back, and put this whole terrible last year behind him.

It was also the third week of dating Nell. Nell, who he was

now one hundred percent, irretrievably in love with. He would tell her, as soon as this week was over, and hope she felt a fraction of the same feeling.

But even if she did feel the same way, she was complex, difficult to read, and she hid her emotions better than anyone he'd met. She cared for him, that much was clear, and their chemistry was explosive. But it might take a long time for her to fall in love.

He could wait for her. As long as she didn't shut him out, he'd keep searching for the little things that opened her up, like a lock springing open when the tumblers clicked into the correct order. She might not trust her own feelings, but they existed.

Once he was past his anxiety problem of the last month, over it for good, he'd be able to take her out, do all the things he hadn't been able to do so far. Then, he'd finally be well enough, good enough for this relationship to happen.

* * *

Nell greeted him at her doorway that night with a quick kiss, keeping the door angled so Marco couldn't see their lips meet. It was torture now, pretending they were friends. No hugs or cuddles, no kisses, and definitely no smelling her hair.

Just friends, he reminded himself as he stepped inside, carrying a cardboard box wrapped in blue paper tucked under his arm.

"I hope you don't mind, I brought him a gift," he said.

Nell narrowed her eyes at him in mock annoyance. "Is that

what I think it is?"

"It might be."

Marco came skidding around the corner, his socks sliding on the linoleum entryway. "Ben. Guess what I found yesterday."

"More geodes?" he guessed.

"Not even that. I think it might be a fossil. But Mom isn't sure. You need to look at it."

"I'd be glad to."

Marco's eyes caught on the box. "Is that a present? Is it for my mom?"

"It's for you, actually. Would you like to take it to the living room to open it up?"

Marco grabbed the box and ran down the hallway to the living room.

Ben used the opportunity to snag Nell around the waist and kiss her, hard and full of need. She broke away a few seconds later, flushed.

"I missed you," he said softly.

"Me too."

"Tell me about your day. Did you have a lot of deliveries?"

"Not more than usual. Lots of spring bouquets going out. And we're planning wedding flowers with a couple who came in the other day. They decided to get married on short notice— in just two weeks. Kind of romantic."

"That sounds fun."

"It is. I liked showing them all the color combinations, and the different floral arrangements they could choose from."

"And the manager's job? The one you told me about the other day. Have you filled out the application yet?"

She paused for a split second, her eyes shifting away from his. "No. I ... Not yet. I'm still not sure."

"You'll know when you're ready," he said, keeping his tone light.

She was lying, and she was good at it, too. No one else might have noticed. But there'd been a hint of vulnerability on her face—there one second, gone the next. She was afraid of rejection. And that was understandable, given her past.

Marco interrupted them by running back into the kitchen, carrying the large plexiglass case with shelving inside. Ben had assembled it before wrapping it up. Marco had already put several of his geodes and other rocks inside, along with some dinosaur figurines. Marco bobbled the case, then righted it at the last second.

"Let's set this down, so we can take a look at it." Ben guided him to the dining room table, while Nell went to the kitchen to stir something on the stove.

"Th-thank you. I needed a place to put all my rocks." Marco's face lit up with excitement, and Ben's chest tightened.

"You'll have such a big collection, you'll need another case soon. You'll have to show me when you fill this one up." He looked up to see Nell shaking her head at him from the other room, amusement in her gaze.

"I will. Wait 'til you see this new one." He took off out of the kitchen to get his new fossil, which did in fact turn out to be a fossil.

"You're the only one I've shown my rocks to," Marco told him, when Nell was out of earshot. "I'd never bring them to school in case they got stolen."

Ben frowned. "Do people steal things at your school?"

"Only from me. Because they like to be bullies. Don't tell Mom I said that." Marco's eyes pleaded with him to understand.

"I won't. But why did they steal from you?" Ben fought to keep his voice level, so his sudden surge of anger wouldn't scare Marco.

Marco shrugged. "Because I wouldn't say anything. I d-didn't used to talk at school last year. Not at all."

A familiar mix of tenderness and rage flooded Ben's veins, half-remembered from his childhood days of fending off bullies from Leah.

He'd keep his word to Marco. But if this boy was his, he'd go straight to the school and tell them. He'd make sure it never happened again. But Marco wasn't his, and neither was Nell. Not yet, not really.

Their dinner conversation covered how scientists date rocks, how old were the oldest rocks, and what kinds of dinosaurs might have lived in Missouri. After dinner and Marco's bedtime, when Nell had tucked her son into bed, she joined Ben on the couch.

"It might be a while before he falls asleep," she warned.

"I remember."

"Thank you for the gift. He's always so excited to see you." She looked down at her lap as she spoke.

"Are you worried about that? That he might be getting attached?" He wanted to tell her not to worry. He wasn't planning on letting Marco down. Or her.

"Not worried, exactly. I guess it makes me realize how much he needs more than just me. As a single mom, I try to be everything to him. But I can't do that."

"No one can be more than one person."

"I know that, in my mind. In reality, I've had to at least try to do it all. There wasn't any other choice."

"Nell. You have to know I want to be there for you. For both of you." The words spilled out of him, too close to what he wanted to say, and not quite enough.

She drew in a breath. "It's almost the end of the three weeks."

"I am very aware of that fact."

"And we haven't talked about what we'll do next. When the trial run is over."

His heart rate accelerated. "My anxiety is better. I haven't had a panic attack in a week. If I can keep it under control, like it is now …"

She shook her head. "You know I don't care about that. I'd want you either way, whether you're having more or less anxiety."

"What if I never got any better? You'd want a partner who couldn't go places like a restaurant or a show? A person who had a hard time going for a walk?"

Her eyes met his, solemn and glinting gray. "I would want that person, if that person was you."

Ben shut his eyes for a moment, swallowing past the burning lump in his throat. "Not like that. I need to be well to be with you, to be there for you. If you can ever trust me enough to let me."

Nell pulled him into her arms and he went, burying his face in her neck, where her smell was sweetest.

Her voice was a soft vibration against his forehead. "I'd be willing to keep trying, after this week. If you are. I … care about you, Ben."

It was enough for now, that she'd admitted a sliver of feeling for him. Ben kissed her softly instead of replying, because if he replied, he'd say he loved her, and she wouldn't be ready to say it back. No words were good enough for her, anyway.

Later, after Marco was asleep, Ben made love to her, like he'd done almost every night this week. This was his person, the only one who'd ever made him feel. She couldn't say it yet, but she must feel the connection, the same as he felt it, a live wire inside his chest attached to her.

Afterward, he held her tight, part of him unable to believe it could be this easy, and he would get to keep her after all. He stroked her hair and pressed kisses to the top of her head.

Maybe that was why, as she fell asleep against him, he didn't wake her this time. He didn't want this to end. He shut his eyes and let himself drift, with the woman he loved right where she was supposed to be, in his arms.

Chapter 17

Nell woke up with the covers rumpled on one side of the bed and no memory of Ben leaving last night. She must have fallen asleep, and hadn't woken up when he'd left. She'd slept hard for eight hours, and it was after 7:00 already.

She stopped dead at the bottom of the staircase. Ben and Marco sat at the dining room table, Marco eating a waffle and watching a documentary on his tablet. The waffle had been cut into little squares, the same way she normally did it for her son.

Ben was watching the show, too, but he jumped up from the table when Nell came in, a guilty look on his face.

"I'm sorry," he blurted.

Marco glanced up from the show. "Mom, Ben accidentally fell asleep on the couch last night. So he made me breakfast while you slept."

Nell looked back and forth between Ben and her son, then turned on her heel and walked out of the room, heart racing.

She placed a hand on her chest, rubbing the center of it.

Ben followed close behind her.

"I'm sorry," he repeated. "I woke up at 6:00 and tried to sneak out the door, but he came downstairs. I was on the couch putting on my shoes, and I made up an excuse. You're upset, I can tell."

"I'm not upset." Was there a word for how she felt right now? Terrified. That was a word. "Did you stay here overnight on purpose? After I fell asleep?"

"I didn't think about it too long. I was sleepy, and I—"

"You let yourself stay here." When he knew she wasn't ready. Her heart refused to slow, pounding against her ribcage.

"Not on purpose. I wouldn't do that. But after our conversation last night, I did … I hoped things were changing. We'd decided to keep seeing each other. I know you didn't want Marco to find out about us yet. I don't think he knows."

"No." She folded her arms tightly across her chest. "I don't think he realizes, either."

"I know we didn't talk about this part last night. I'm sorry."

Nell studied his face, the earnest, pleading eyes. She did believe him. He'd never been anything but honest with her.

"It's okay. I don't blame you."

She shut her eyes, reaching for calm. Beyond her initial shocked reaction to seeing Ben in her kitchen this morning, there'd been something else. A rush of longing that had almost knocked her over. This morning was dangerously close to what she'd always wished for, and it would be too easy to believe it was real.

Her feelings for Ben were complicated, and she wasn't ready to put a name on them. She definitely hadn't been ready for him to make Marco's breakfast.

"Tell me what you want me to do. Should I go now?" Ben's voice was soft, but it held a thread of worry.

"No. You can stay." She shook her head to clear it. "Like you said, he doesn't suspect anything. Do you want some coffee?"

"Okay." He gave her a long look. "If you're sure."

"I'm sure. I was surprised, that's all. I wasn't ready to see you here in the morning."

"I understand. Next time, we'll plan it. Whenever you want it to happen."

"Of course." Nell fixed a smile on her face. "Maybe after we both have coffee, this will seem more normal."

"Coffee always helps," he said. Still, he seemed to be analyzing her, and she turned her face away from his probing gaze.

"I'll only stay a few minutes," he added. "I have to leave to get ready for work anyway."

"And I have to get Marco out the door in forty-five minutes."

In the kitchen, Nell scooped coffee grounds into the coffee maker. Marco had finished his breakfast, and he paused his video to launch himself into a conversation with Ben about the show he'd been watching. He gestured wildly, almost knocking his plate to the ground. Ben caught it at the last minute and slid it away from his flailing elbows, then looked up and winked at Nell.

Nell turned her back on them both for a minute, facing the counter. She needed to pull herself together, but tears stung her eyes and her throat burned.

So it felt like Ben belonged here. So he was perfect with her son, and perfect in bed, and perfect for her.

Last night, they'd agreed to keep dating. She should be ecstatic things were working out in a way she'd never dared to hope. So why was she shaking all over? It was too much, too good. It couldn't be real, that was the problem with it.

She took a steadying breath and reached above her head to the cabinet to get mugs, setting them on the counter one by one with care. She poured the coffee with a shaking hand.

"How do you take your coffee?" she asked. She'd never seen him at breakfast, so she didn't know. There were so many things she still didn't know about him, all different ways things could go wrong.

"Black is fine." His dark eyes met hers, seeing through her, like always. He stood and crossed the kitchen to her.

"Thank you for the coffee," he said softly. "But I should get going. Let you get ready for your day."

A buzzing sound interrupted him, and he frowned and pulled his phone out of his pocket. The frown deepened when he scanned the screen for the caller's name.

"I need to take this."

He strode out of the kitchen, answering the call in a low voice as he walked into the front entryway. He paced back and forth as he talked to whoever was on the other end. She could hear his side of the conversation, but it was all one-word answers given in a clipped tone of voice. Maybe another patient emergency.

Nell opened her own phone and scanned through her messages. Her email inbox contained several junk messages. And one reply, from her job application for the manager position at the plant nursery—a polite rejection letter, saying she didn't have the necessary qualifications for the job, but to please consider them for future applications.

She clicked her phone off and set it on the counter. She hadn't expected an interview. It had been a very long shot, and she hadn't gotten it. Just one more rejection to move past. It was a good thing she hadn't told Ben, because now she wouldn't have to explain.

When Ben didn't return to the kitchen after a few more minutes, she poked her head out the door to check on him.

He was leaning against the wall by her front door, one hand on the middle of his chest. His breathing was short, labored, his face a pale gray color. She rushed over to him.

"Ben, is it a panic attack? Can you sit down for a minute?"

His head whipped around. "I'm fine. Go back to Marco."

"Marco will be okay without me for a minute. Please, sit. I don't want you to pass out." She reached out to put a hand on his upper arm, but he jerked away from her. A moment later, he slid down the wall, knees bent up to his chest. His head dropped forward, but his breath didn't slow, continuing to puff out of him as if he'd run a mile. She'd never seen him this bad.

She lowered herself to the floor next to him, not touching him, but sitting cross-legged by his side.

"I wish … you would go." He squeezed his eyes shut. Sweat had broken out across his forehead.

She shook her head. "I won't leave you alone like this. Can I put a hand on your back?"

After a pause, he nodded. She placed a hand between his shoulder blades, resting it there. His heart galloped under her palm.

"I need … to go home." He made a move to stand, and she stopped him with a hand on his arm.

"Not yet. Ben, you can't drive like this. I know you want to be in your own space. I can drive you, if you want me to. But don't get in your car like this."

"I hate this." He squeezed his eyes shut.

"I know. I hate it for you."

With her free hand, she caught his hand and laced her fingers between his. He squeezed her with surprising force, shut his eyes, and started taking deep breaths, slowing his exhales with a breathing exercise. After a minute, his heart rate slowed under her hand.

Marco chose that moment to come out of the kitchen. He stopped in his tracks when he saw them on the floor together.

"Mom? Is Ben s-sick?" he asked, his voice high with uncertainty.

Ben looked up at her, and she drew back at the expression of anguish on his face.

"Get him out of here. Please. I don't want to scare him."

She gave a quick nod, got up from her spot on the floor, and went to her son.

"Ben isn't feeling good, but he's going to be okay. We need to leave him alone for a minute, so he can have some privacy."

Marco's face screwed up with confusion. "We shouldn't leave someone alone when they need help."

"Sometimes, people need to be by themselves. I promise he'll be okay." She tried to usher Marco back toward the kitchen, but he slipped past her and ran upstairs. His bedroom door banged shut.

Ben struggled to his feet. He was unsteady, but better than he had been a few minutes ago.

"I need to go." He scanned around the entryway for his jacket, found it, and yanked one sleeve on, then the other.

"Ben, please wait a few more minutes, until you're more calm."

"I'm fine." He wouldn't meet her eyes.

"What happened? Is something going on at work? Do you need help?"

He drew in an unsteady inhale. "I guess you'll end up seeing this anyway." He thumbed open his phone and handed it to her.

The screen showed an article from the city newspaper's weekend magazine. The headline read: "Local Doctor Back in Office, and in Bloom."

Nell scanned the first few sentences.

Flowers are good for your mental health. Just ask local psychologist Ben Friedman, who is taking in-person appointments again following an extended absence. Social media posts showing patients with their flower arrangements brought a new focus on the clinic, which has been nominated for a national award in mental health care. Clinic patients were surprised and delighted by the floral deliveries, and the return of their doctor.

The article went on for a few more paragraphs—a feel-good piece about the clinic that would no doubt bring a lot of new patients in. And it had devastated Ben.

Nell looked up at him, eyes widening with realization. "Your patients didn't know. About you being gone."

"No." He shook his head. "I mean, individually, they knew they hadn't seen me in person for a while. But I think most of them hadn't made the connection that I'd been absent. Until the flowers."

"But the article doesn't say why you were gone. It doesn't reveal any personal information."

"I know. But people talk. They'll know something's wrong with me." His head dropped. "I thought I had the situation under control. That I was back to normal, or at least close to it. But I'm not."

"You don't have to tell them anything." A surge of protective anger washed through her. He'd fought so hard for the progress he'd made.

"I'm not better, though. Look what just happened."

"You are better," she said fiercely. "I've seen it with my own eyes, even if I'm the only person who knew what you were going through."

His expression softened, looking at her with a wistful sadness. "You were the only person who knew, until recently. And you were so supportive."

She didn't like him using the past tense in that sentence. "And I'll keep supporting you. You'll get past this."

He shook his head. "I should have known I wasn't ready for a relationship. It was wishful thinking on my part. I just … wanted you so much. But I need to keep working on myself, until I'm all the way better."

He let out a short, bitter laugh. "When I suggested the three-week trial run for us dating, I thought it was because you needed time to be sure, to be ready. I should have known it would be me who couldn't do it."

Nell's hand flew to her throat. "Are you saying—"

She was interrupted by Marco running down the stairs. He was too quick for her, dodging past her legs and running up to Ben. He slipped something into Ben's jacket pocket and ran back upstairs.

"I'm sorry about that," she said. "What did he put in there?"

Ben's face twisted as he pulled Marco's geode, the first one he'd found, out of his pocket. The clear crystal caught the morning sunlight coming in the window.

"I can't take this from him." Ben placed the rock on the end table by the front door. "I'm sorry. I'm so sorry for disappointing him. Both of you."

He turned away from her and reached for the door handle.

"You're really breaking up with me." Nell's voice sounded wooden, hollow. Earlier in the morning, she'd been on the verge of tears, but now she felt nothing. No feelings at all.

Ben paused, his hand on the door. "I guess, technically, we were never dating." His voice was tight, clipped. "It was a test. And it didn't work out, because I'm not well. I'm sorry."

Ben straightened his spine, drew his shoulders back. The rigid stranger she'd met four weeks ago was back. No sign of the kind, sensitive man she'd gotten to know and maybe could have even loved.

He didn't love her.

And she wasn't in love with him. She wasn't sad, or angry, or anything else as Ben pulled open her front door and walked out of it. The door shut behind him with a click, ending things between them. All things had to end, but especially good things, the things you'd pinned some hopes on.

She bolted the lock and didn't linger by the door. It was time to get Marco ready for school, and she had dishes to do before she got dressed. A full slate of deliveries to go out this morning. Nothing like routine to keep you on track, and she wouldn't be late today.

Chapter 18

On the sixth day after the newspaper article came out, Ben paced back and forth in his living room, phone in his hand. He'd almost texted Nell a dozen times this morning, but each time he'd stopped himself.

He hadn't left the house since coming home from her place a week ago. He'd gotten himself in the front door, called Cameron, and canceled all his in-person appointments. Then he'd stopped answering his phone. Calls came in from the clinic, presumably to talk about the article, and he'd let them all go to voicemail.

The one thing he'd wanted to avoid had happened, his worst fear manifested, in the way phobias had of showing their faces, just when you thought things were safe. Now, not only had he failed to defeat his anxiety, he'd failed to hide it from the world.

People would assume something was wrong with him, after reading that article. They might even think he had a serious physical illness, but then, he couldn't correct them because they'd want to know what else it was.

And on top of his complete failure in the mental health department was the way he'd failed Nell. Her frozen face, the way she'd stood, still and quiet, when he told her they weren't dating anymore. That they never had been. He'd hurt her in the worst way possible, leaving her exactly the way she'd been left before.

Marco's horrified expression also wouldn't leave his mind. He'd been scared, and Ben had been the cause of it.

And that was one more reason he couldn't be around them, couldn't be close to them anymore. He couldn't have a breakdown if he was helping take care of a child. He had to be able to hold things together, be strong enough to take care of someone else.

After seeing his massive panic attack, Nell had to know it was the best choice for them to be apart. He'd thought he was getting better, but he wasn't. Maybe he never would.

His phone buzzed with a text and he hurled it onto the couch and continued pacing. She'd said she would support him still. But how could she mean that?

I would want that person, if that person was you, she'd said.

Bitter guilt made his breath come shorter. He wanted her still, with a deep ache that wouldn't go away, no matter how much he ran on the treadmill or buried himself in research for his next writing project.

Even though he wasn't well enough to be with her, it didn't stop his stupid heart from loving her.

The night before, he'd lit yahrzeit candles at sundown to mark the anniversary of Leah's death. He'd watched the candles burn and remembered her silly laugh, her sense of humor, and how her face lit up every time he visited. How he'd loved taking care of her.

After saying a Hebrew blessing for the candles, he'd said a few words just for her, reaching for their connection.

"Leah. I know you wouldn't want me to be like this. I fell apart a little bit, after you left. I always tried so hard to hold everything together for you. But maybe I had to fall apart, so I could be put back together in a different way. This new version of me will always have a hole in the shape of you, though."

With his eyes on the flame, he focused on memories of them reading books together, their long walks and conversations. When the candles went out, he'd gone up to bed, and woken this morning feeling ready to consider what he'd done a week ago.

He couldn't fix it, but he could at least stand to think about it, where before today, he'd shoved it as far out of his mind as possible.

His phone buzzed again, muffled against the couch cushion. He grabbed it, saw Vanessa's name on the screen, and swiped right to answer the call before he could think better of it.

"What."

"I'm coming over there. Now. You better be wearing pants." She hung up on him.

Ben frowned down at himself. Of course he was fully dressed. No matter how bad things got, he got dressed in the morning.

Twenty minutes later, his doorbell rang. Vanessa shoved past him, staggering under the weight of several canvas shopping bags with the handles looped over her arms. In her hands, she cradled two potted plants, which she set on his kitchen counter before rounding on him.

Her face was red with exertion and irritation, and her sharp green eyes pinned him in place.

"What is all this?" he asked.

"Shut up and listen to me for a few minutes without interrupting. I know you already think you've got this situation all figured out. But you haven't been in the clinic the last week, so therefore, you know nothing."

"Okay." Ben shut his mouth, staring at her. Vanessa in full fury mode was something he'd rarely witnessed.

"'All this' is a fraction of what's been pouring into the clinic." She lifted one of the canvas bags and upended it onto his kitchen floor. Several dozen cards, letters, and wrapped gifts fell out of it, sliding to the floor with a swish.

"And this." She dumped out the next bag. "And all of these." With a flourish, she tossed the empty bags to the floor. A few cards skittered under the cabinets.

"Are those …"

"For you? Yes. They're all for you. Would you like me to read you one? No, don't answer that. I will." She bent and picked up a random card, opening it with a fingernail.

"'Dear Dr. Friedman, I'm so glad you've been able to return to work. Wishing you all the best.' Here's another. 'You have our support, no matter what you're going through. We are thinking of you and sending our love.'"

"Stop." Ben held up a hand. "I get it."

He cleared his throat. "It was very kind of people to send those. But I never wanted them to know in the first place. I don't want their pity."

She glared at him. "It's not pity. It's called support. It's what people do when they care about one another." She planted her hands on her hips. "Did it never occur to you that people would support you, as much as you've supported them all these years?"

"I—"

"And you teach them how to take care of themselves, but you refuse to do the same for yourself."

He looked over her shoulder, out his kitchen window to avoid her gaze. "That thought had occurred to me lately. And not just about me. All of us need to take better care of ourselves."

"Then listen to yourself. So you have problems, like the rest of the world does. What kind of example are you setting, shoving all your own issues down like this and hiding away in your house?"

"I know." His voice came out sharper than he'd intended. "I know that's what I'm doing. But I can't do anything else. I tried to get better, and I failed. I read that stupid article and had a massive panic attack in front of Nell and her son. The worst I'd had in months. I really thought…" He swallowed. "I thought I was dying."

"Oh, Ben." Her voice softened.

"And I've been taking my medicine and doing my breathing exercises and none of it worked. It's… I'm afraid it's stronger than me. I'll never get better." His voice broke off. Vanessa stayed silent, waiting for more.

"I broke up with her," he added.

"No. You didn't. Ben, you did not. Not because of a panic attack."

"What else could I do? I'm not well enough to be with anyone right now. I'm not even sure I can go outside without it happening all over again."

She raised a brow at him. "Have you been outside since that day?"

"No."

"But you were, before. You were going to work every day. You were absolutely making progress. You're not in the same place as you were a month ago."

"I might be. I might be right back where I started." He shoved a hand through his hair, grinding his palm against his forehead. "I'm sorry. I know I'm not making sense. I don't know what would happen now, if I tried going out. I think I didn't want to find out."

Vanessa picked her way through the pile of cards on the floor, her pointed heels stabbing holes in a couple of the envelopes.

When she got close, she put a tentative hand on his forearm. "Would you like to find out, with a friend?"

He looked up, finally meeting her eyes. There was no judgment in them, only kindness. "Yes. I think I could do that."

He followed her out the front door. She sat on the bench on his porch, the one where he'd sat with Nell after she'd dropped the flowers. Vanessa patted the cushion next to her, and he sat.

His neighborhood was peaceful this time of morning, with everyone already at work. Birds sang in the branches, and a brisk breeze swirled around them, lifting Vanessa's hair.

He felt normal. No panic attack, no accelerated breathing or heart rate.

He drew in a shaky breath. "I made a mistake, didn't I? A really big mistake."

Vanessa nodded in agreement, gazing out onto his street with a serene expression. "Yes, you did. But the good news is, some mistakes are fixable."

"What do I do? What can I say to her, after what I did?"

She patted him on the shoulder. "I can't tell you that. You'll figure out the best thing. But maybe I'll see you at work next week?"

"Yes. I'll call and let Cameron know. And Vanessa … I've been meaning to ask you if you'll come with me to Chicago. To accept the award, if we win it."

Her brow furrowed. "But why? There's no need for both of us to go."

"I think there is. For one thing, you started the clinic with me. You've been just as instrumental in its success as I have. You've been running the place alone without me this month. The social media posts were your idea, even if they led to that stupid newspaper article."

"That stupid article brought in a dozen new patients last week."

"It didn't."

"It did. I'm telling you, people care about you. And they like seeing the clinic as a place where doctors care about their patients as people. It's going to save our business."

Ben processed that for a moment. "That's really good news."

"It is." She gave a knowing nod.

"But about the trip. There's another reason I'd like you to come. I'm doing what you said, and I'm asking for help. I don't think I'd like to travel alone right now."

Her smile lit her whole face. "I'd love to go with you. That would be … very nice."

He watched from his place on the porch as Vanessa got into her car, gave him a wave, and drove off.

Back inside his house, he eyed the mess of cards and plants and gifts. In the middle of his kitchen counter stood the ficus tree Nell had given him, bright green and sporting several new leaves.

She'd been right. The thing kept growing, no matter how

little sunlight it got.

* * *

Ben always advised his patients, when making an apology, to do four things. One, offer an explanation, but no excuses. Two, be sincere in your regret. Third, ask for forgiveness. And last, tell the person what changes you plan to make in the future.

He could do all of the first three without a problem, but he was stuck on the fourth. What could he tell Nell he'd do differently in the future? He'd keep taking his medicine, but beyond that, what could he offer? That they'd just have to hope he never got worse again? Because he might. He'd lived with anxiety all his life, and now he knew how bad it could get. What could he promise to do for her, if that happened?

On an airplane, they told you to secure your own oxygen mask before trying to help others, but he'd always tried to help others first. And he was the one who'd needed assistance all this time.

Maybe the reason he'd walked out on Nell was that he hadn't fully admitted, to anyone, that he wasn't okay.

At his desk, he drafted two letters. One was an open letter to his patients, which he would send out in the clinic's weekly newsletter. In it, he gave a brief explanation of why he'd been absent. Without telling them every detail, he let them know he'd been struggling with anxiety issues. He concluded the letter:

Thank you for your support, which means the world to me. It's

*one thing to talk about needing community, and another thing to
experience it. I'm humbled by how much our clinic's community
cares for one another. It's what makes The Well Space so special.*

The second letter he directed to the staff of the clinic, con-
taining a slightly different message. He outlined a couple of
employee policy changes which might raise eyebrows, but
which would be the best thing for everyone.

He made several phone calls. A plan had formed in his head,
a way he could apologize and ask for help and show Nell how
much he loved her. That she was needed, and it was safe for
her to trust him again.

She could depend on him now, because he'd admitted his
own limitations, and it hadn't broken him after all. It had made
him stronger.

But he was impatient. A week without hearing her voice had
weakened his resolve. He dialed her number. It rang multiple
times before going to voicemail. At the sound of her bright
voice in the recorded message, he drew in a sharp breath, pain
and regret lancing him again.

"This is Nell. I'm sorry I missed your call, but I'll return it as
soon as I can. Have a wonderful day."

She wouldn't return his call, and he didn't blame her. He'd
hurt her, the one person in the world he should never hurt. If
she didn't accept his apology ... He wouldn't let himself think
that far.

Chapter 19

Nell hauled a large floral centerpiece out the front door of the shop to the van. The pink and white roses smacked her in the face as she walked, and their thick, sweet scent screamed "wedding."

Some people found the love of their lives and got engaged and married in two weeks, and some people didn't. Some people had to carry on and take care of everything alone, and that was fine, too.

She was so tired, though. The last two weeks, doing her daily routine had felt like slogging through thick mud. Getting out of bed, driving Marco to school, going through the motions at work—all of it left her exhausted. She couldn't shake it off and put on her usual smile as well as she had before.

She didn't let herself think about the reason. Men were unreliable, they left you, and she should have learned that lesson and learned it well six years ago. Never assume you knew a man well enough to trust him, and never assume he had your best interests at heart.

Chapter 19

She slammed the van door shut with more force than necessary, turned, and found Amy standing behind her, arms folded across her chest.

"Careful." Amy nodded toward the back of the van. "I don't think those flowers did anything to you."

"I'm sorry. I loaded them in the back gently, I promise."

"Sit down for a minute. Let's chat." Amy gestured to the bumper of the van, and they sat on the edge, feet propped on the curb.

"Is there anything going on I should know about?" Amy asked. "I've learned I can't make assumptions with you. Thanks for bringing back those ferns, by the way. They look amazing." The corner of her mouth lifted in a little smile.

Nell looked down at her sneakers. "It's no problem. They didn't like the pots they were in, so I switched them out and gave them time to adjust."

"So. You've been pretty quiet lately."

"I didn't get the manager job," Nell admitted. "The one you told me about. I applied for it, but they said I wasn't qualified."

Amy frowned. "I'm sorry. Maybe I shouldn't have told you about that, or encouraged you to apply. But I thought you had a good shot, for what it's worth."

"I guess I didn't, after all."

"And what about your college application? You said you might be finishing your degree this year."

Nell planted her face in her hands. "I got the scholarship."

"I'm sorry. Your voice was muffled, but did you just say you got a scholarship?"

She lifted her head to look at her boss. "Yes. I found out yesterday. I applied for a scholarship for students who're the first person in their family to go to college. And I got it. Full tuition."

"Congratulations. That's great news." Amy clapped her on the back.

Nell shook her head. "I can't take it, though. I can't go back to school now."

"What are you talking about? You have to take it."

"I need to find more hours to work, not less. If I enroll in even one college class, I'd have to take two mornings off a week. Some of the classes are available in the evenings, but most aren't. And the scholarship doesn't apply to online students. I don't think I can pull it off. But it's fine."

She jumped up from the back of the van. "I'd better get going. No one wants their wedding flowers delivered late."

"Wait." Amy's voice stopped her from rounding the side of the van. "Don't turn down the scholarship yet, okay? I want to help you brainstorm some solutions. It seems like a shame to waste the opportunity."

"You don't have to remind me. And it's really nice of you to want to help. I guess I need two or three of me to get everything done." She forced out a hollow-sounding laugh. "I might be starting another part-time job next week. I have an interview after work today."

Amy frowned. "And when were you going to tell me that?" She put a hand on her hip, exasperated. "Never mind. Look, when you get back from this delivery, come to my office. We'll talk about this some more."

"Okay." Nell didn't see the point in talking about it any more, but she agreed, to get Amy off her back.

"And there's nothing else going on with you?" Amy squinted at her, examining her face.

Nell cut her gaze away. "No. Nothing else."

Amy drew in a deep breath, as if reaching for patience. "All right. See you later, then." She marched away, muttering to herself. "Stubborn, secretive …"

Well, so what if she was secretive. Not everything needed to be shared. Sharing too much of yourself was a recipe for problems.

When Nell arrived at the delivery address, the bride and groom were overjoyed with their floral arrangements. The bright happiness on their faces as they looked at one another made Nell's chest ache. She was very careful with the floral arrangements as she unloaded them. Some plants held particular importance.

When she got back to Tillie's Flowers, she parked the van, hung up the keys, and went to the back to look for Amy. Thirty minutes later, she emerged from Amy's office in a daze.

"Thank you, again," she said from the doorway.

Amy nodded curtly. "Of course. You can shut that on your way out."

Nell made it to her car, put the key in the ignition, but didn't start it. She sat in the parking lot, staring out the windshield.

Amy had promoted her to assistant manager and given her a raise. Enough of a raise that she could afford not to work a third job. And she would have flexible hours, to accommodate taking one college class per semester at the university.

Amy had also called her friend at the nursery. He'd agreed to interview Nell for the job in six months, after she'd completed part of her coursework toward finishing her degree.

For once, something was going her way. After years of life beating her up, she'd finally had the courage to try for something more, and it had worked out. She would finish college. It might take longer than a year, but she had a plan.

Goosebumps rose on her arms.

If only she could tell Mom about this. But there was no one to share her good news with. Ben had been the one to find the scholarship and send her the information. He'd been the one to encourage her, the one who'd believed she could do it. At every step of their relationship, he'd built her up. Until that last day.

He would want to know about this. He'd called her once last week, and she'd stared at the phone in her hand as it rang and went to voicemail. He hadn't left a message.

She tossed her phone in the cupholder and started her car. The less she thought about Ben, the better she'd feel.

And one person would be happy to hear her news, even if he didn't entirely understand what it meant. She headed out of the parking lot and drove to Marco's school.

* * *

That night, she took Marco out to dinner to celebrate, a rare splurge. Their favorite restaurant was a local old-fashioned diner, where Marco always ordered the same thing—a cheeseburger and french fries. The waitress brought them a pack of crayons, and Marco colored his paper placemat while he waited for dinner.

"I don't know why you're excited to go back to school," he said. "Grownups are lucky because they don't have to go to school."

"But college is different. Grownups get to learn about things they're excited about. Imagine if you got to go to school and only learn about dinosaurs all day."

Marco's eyes lit up. "That would be cool."

"I get to learn about plants in my classes. Plus, college isn't all day. I'll only go to class two days a week, and only for an hour or so. I still have to work."

"And you'll still pick me up from school, right?" He peeled the crayon wrapper back with his fingernail.

"Of course. I'll still do all the normal things I do with you."

Marco's shoulders relaxed. "That's okay, then."

"And when I'm done with my college classes, I'll be able to get a better job. One that will pay more money. I could quit working at the coffee shop, and then we'd have the whole weekend together."

"Saturday and Sunday?"

"Yep."

Marco processed that as he filled in colors on a cartoon character. "I want to go to the park to look for rocks this weekend."

She took a deep breath, reaching for calm. "Don't you want to do something else? We could go see a movie. There's a new superhero movie out this weekend."

The last two weekends, all Marco had wanted to do was look for rocks. At least he hadn't mentioned Ben again this week.

After Ben had left, Nell explained to Marco that he wasn't feeling well, and they might not see him again for a while. For the first week, Marco kept asking what had happened, when they'd see Ben again, and why he'd left. After Nell gave him the same explanation over and over, he'd seemed to give up.

"I don't like movies." He put down the crayon and fiddled with the sugar packets on the table. "Except documentaries."

"Or we could check out that new trampoline place. You'd

like jumping."

"No. No, thank you," he corrected himself, shaking his head.

The waitress arrived with their dinner and set down both plates. Marco took a huge bite, chewed, and swallowed.

"My display case is almost full now. So we need to call Ben."

Nell was so startled to hear Ben's name after a week, it took her a moment to reply.

"What do you mean?"

"Ben said he wanted to see my collection when the case was full. So I've been working on filling it up, and now we have to show him."

"Oh." Nell covered her eyes with her hand, taking a steadying breath. According to Marco's seven year-old logic, if he filled up the display case, he'd get to see Ben again.

She met his serious gaze. "You really want to see him again, don't you?"

Marco nodded vigorously.

"Sweetie. I can't promise we'll see him again. The truth is, he said … He told me he wasn't going to come over to our house for a while." She couldn't bring herself to say never. "This is not your fault at all. But he might not be able to come. I'm sure he'd love to see your rocks, if he could."

Marco frowned. "Why won't he come over? He likes both of us."

Nell's heart constricted. Damn Ben for making her have to explain this to Marco, for letting down her son as well. This was exactly what she'd wanted to avoid all along. At least Marco still didn't know they'd been dating.

"I think he's having some personal problems, and he didn't feel like he could handle them right now."

"Oh." Marco took another bite, frowning as he chewed. "It's

because he's shy. And nervous. I told him I'm like that at school sometimes, too."

"So you understand why we can't call him right now."

"Not really."

But Marco let the topic go while they finished their dinner.

That night, after she'd tucked him in and taken care of all her plants, Nell sat alone at her kitchen table, staring at her phone. It would be so easy to call or text Ben, to give in to the urge to find out how he was doing. Was he having more panic attacks now? Had his clinic gotten a lot of attention, following the newspaper article?

It was none of her concern anymore. And yet her heart reached out to him, as if they were tied together by a thread that had stretched thin, but not snapped. When she closed her eyes at night, she saw his glittering dark eyes, gazing at her with an emotion that had felt so real at the time.

And her feelings for him … She wouldn't name them. She wouldn't call it love, because if it had been love, she'd be heartbroken right now. And she was not heartbroken. She was thriving, and going back to college, and doing everything she'd forgotten she wanted to do for six long years.

If Ben loved her, he wouldn't have left. But that's what he'd done.

After brushing her teeth and changing into pajamas, she eyed her empty bed. She'd barely slept the last two weeks. She dragged the covers off and pulled them into Marco's room, like she used to do, when they were first alone together. She made a nest on the floor next to his bed and curled up inside it.

Pulling the covers over her head, she tried to calm down enough to fall asleep. She hugged a pillow to her chest, but she did not pretend it was Ben. And she did not cry.

Chapter 20

"Mom. Mommy. Wake up." Marco jumped on the pile of blankets she'd slept in and ripped the covers back from her face and shoulders.

She bolted upright. "What's wrong? What happened?"

"Outside. You have to look outside. There's so m-many colors. Why are they doing that?" He grabbed her hand and tugged.

She scrambled to stand. "Doing what? What's going on?"

"I don't know. Come s-see. You need to look out the kitchen window. I was making cereal and I looked out there and I saw them."

He held her hand as they rushed to the kitchen. Her breath caught when she pulled the curtain aside.

A fairy garden had replaced her barren front yard. Bright red and yellow tulips lined the walkways, where a fresh layer of mulch had been laid down. A row of flowering rose bushes lined the front of the property, a riot of peach, yellow, and crimson. A flowerbed had been planted by each front door in the row of houses, with irises, daffodils, and greenery. They'd even put an archway at the head of the path, with ivy climbing the sides, threaded through a wooden trellis.

"What …" Nell scanned the property, looking for workers. A glint of bright orange hair caught her eye at the north corner of the lawn. Amy. Had she known about this before, and hadn't said anything?

The Tillie's Flowers van was parked at the curb. Inside of it was the shadowed figure of a tall man with dark hair.

"Marco, stay inside, okay?" Nell wrenched open the door and ran outside in her bare feet. She ran across the wet grass toward the van, because she had to know for sure who'd done this, before he disappeared again.

Ben glanced up just in time to see her approach, and he opened the van door at once, unfolding himself from the passenger seat.

Nell stopped dead and wrapped her arms around her middle. Because now that he was here, she had no idea what to say to him. All of him was achingly familiar—the pressed charcoal suit, the black waves brushed back from his face. Dark brown eyes filled with emotion.

"What are you doing here?" The words came out breathless, not nearly as cool or calm as she'd have liked. She looked down at herself and oh, she was wearing sleep shorts and a T-shirt, her feet covered with wet grass. She hadn't even pulled her hair back.

Ben stared at her, looking lost for words for a minute before he found his voice. "I … Nell, I need to apologize to you. I know how much I hurt you, and leaving you that day was the last thing I should have done. At the time, I thought it was the right thing to do, but that is not an excuse for how I behaved."

He cleared his throat and squared his shoulders, as if reciting the rest of a set of words he'd memorized. "I hope someday, you can forgive me, but I know it might not be possible for a long time, if ever. In the future—"

"I get that you're apologizing to me. I really do. You're sorry you left."

"So sorry. I've wished a hundred times I could go back and not say those things to you."

"Well, now you've said you're sorry." She stared down at her toes and tried to hang on to the bare minimum of civility. "And the flowers are very beautiful. Thank you."

"You're welcome." Ben looked uncomfortable as hell, and that was fine because she'd been uncomfortable the whole time she'd known him. He'd cracked her open, filled in all her empty spaces, and then abandoned her.

Her breath picked up, and her eyes burned, but this was not the time to break down, because he shouldn't matter that much, sorry or not. He wasn't staying. In a few minutes, he'd drive off and go back to his life, satisfied he'd made amends.

She tipped her head back and squinted up at him. "So why are you here? You could have said all that in a voicemail. Why did you come back?"

"Why did I—" Ben's face twisted. "I'm such an idiot, for not saying this part first. Nell. I came back because I love you. I loved you then, and I do now. You are the love of my life, and I never thought I'd get to have that. And it's okay if you don't feel the same way, or if you're not sure. But I had to do something, when I realized what a huge mistake I'd made. I had to show you— Sweetheart, no. Please don't cry."

But she couldn't stop crying. As soon as he'd said the word "love," huge, gulping sobs racked her shoulders. Ben pulled her into his arms and held her close, his hand stroking her back.

"I love you too. Ben, I love you," she managed between hiccuping breaths.

His hand froze on her back. "You love me."

"I do. I didn't realize, but I do." She hadn't recognized the emotion, or hadn't trusted him enough to let herself feel it. She'd been numb for so long. But the sweet ache in the center of her chest was love. It had taken root and bloomed there quietly, without her even knowing its name.

Ben held her until her tears slowed. She took a step back from him, drawing in a steadying breath. "If you ever disappear on me again—"

"I won't. I promise, never again. I know that was the worst possible thing I could have done to you, walking out like that. I thought I had to be a different person to be with you. But it turns out, I was wrong." A huge smile transformed his face. "God, Nell. Really? You love me?"

"I think I do. You'd better kiss me to make sure, though."

His mouth came down on hers, achingly tender and soft. Their surroundings disappeared, and there was only him, the feel of his arms holding her close, and the smell of flowers all around them.

He pulled back after a minute, breathless. "Can we go inside?"

"Yeah, let's go inside." She threaded her arm around his waist and they started up the path to her door. After a few steps, Nell stopped walking and studied her yard. She'd run out the door too fast to pay attention to it before, but these flower arrangements were familiar.

"This garden design … It's from one of my drawings," she said.

"It is. I hope I remembered most of the details."

"You gave me my dream garden."

"Well." He cleared his throat. "I know this is a rental. Your landlord was fine with me providing free landscaping here, but I'd hoped … I mean, someday, you could have your dream garden at my house. Our house. When you're ready, of course."

Nell swiped her eyes with the back of a hand. "Thank you, Ben. So much. I didn't look that closely when I ran out the door. But this is perfect. And you called Amy to arrange it."

He nodded. "Last week. She told me she had some landscaper friends, and she'd work something out. It was beyond the scope of the flower shop, but I wanted her to have part of the profits."

"She knew all last week? Yesterday, she asked me what was going on with me, and I said it was nothing."

"Well. I asked her to keep it a secret. I didn't know what your response would be, but I wanted to be here when you found out."

"I love it. And I think Marco was more excited than me at first. He's the one who spotted them first and woke me up."

On cue, Marco's face appeared in the front window, watching them approach. Nell opened the door, and he came around the corner from the kitchen, staring up at the two of them, his eyes fixed on Ben's arm around Nell's waist.

"Why were you kissing my mom?" he demanded, as shocked as if he'd seen them sprout wings and start flying.

Ben shot a helpless look at Nell. Clearly, he hadn't planned a speech for this part of the morning.

"Ben brought us all these flowers," she told him. "To say he was sorry for the way he left before. He wanted to come back. And he and I are going to try dating now."

Marco wrinkled his nose. "So he was your friend, but now he's your boyfriend."

"That's right."

Marco nodded knowingly, as if everything made sense now. "It's all right. That happened to one of my friends at school, and he said having a girlfriend wasn't as bad as it seemed."

He fixed Ben with a stern look. "You should have come back sooner. Mom was sad."

Ben knelt down by her son. "I'm very sorry. I won't do it again. I already promised your mom, and I promise you, too."

"I told her you were just nervous, like I am at school. But that's okay."

Ben swallowed. "You're right about me being nervous. I'm glad you understand."

"No problem. Hey, I can show you my collection now." He turned and ran upstairs.

Nell shook her head. "All he wants to do is hunt for rocks now. If you're ever up for taking him ..."

Ben straightened and took her hands. "I'd love to. I'll take him every weekend, as long as I'm able. I never wanted to hurt him. You must have been so angry with me, for his sake."

"I think he was confused more than anything else. He kept asking when we could call you."

He shook his head. "I'm never going to stop apologizing. I might need more flowers."

"You can stop now." She smiled up at him, her realest, truest smile. "Because you're back. And you love me."

"Always."

Nell got ready for work upstairs while Ben admired Marco's rock collection. When she came down the stairs, they were seated together, chatting about a rock that Marco was certain was a dinosaur egg.

Ben had made toaster waffles again. He looked up at her and smiled, love in his eyes.

It was a mirror image of the morning two weeks ago, when he'd had his panic attack and left. Only in this version, he stayed. This time, she let herself believe it was real.

She would make a life with this man. They would move in together, maybe not right away, but someday. She would support him and be supported.

The family she'd always wanted was here, not how she'd planned, but better. The things you poured your love into grew and thrived, and she would tend this well.

Chapter 21

Four months later

Ben put a hand up to shield his eyes from the sun and scanned the horizon. From this far up, the landscape stretched for miles in every direction, all rolling green hills and limestone rock faces in this part of the Flint Hills. They'd hiked up from the base of a hill two miles back, and when they returned, they'd have lunch at a bed and breakfast in the nearby town. The day trip was a perfect escape from their daily routine, and it was also perfect for what he had planned next.

When he'd sent out his employee policy changes to his staff a few months ago, he'd said the new rules would be strictly enforced for everyone, and that included himself. All employees had their paid time off doubled, and he required that the time be taken off each year. He'd also purchased a gym and spa membership for everyone, increased their half-hour lunch breaks to an hour, and instituted a half-day schedule on

Fridays. No one had complained about the changes so far.

The staff of The Well Space could only function if they were well themselves, he'd told them in the staff memo. From now on, he expected everyone to prioritize their own health as much as their patients'.

A rustling behind him on the trail made him turn his head. Nell emerged around the corner of the path, cradling a tall, thin plant dotted with buds. She'd wrapped the ball of dirt and roots at the base of the plant in her windbreaker.

Her ponytail swung back and forth as she made her way over to him, and she flashed him a grin that made his chest hurt.

He turned the small velvet box in his pocket over and over between his fingers.

"It's a larkspur," she said, holding up the plant. "I wanted to add it to the garden at home. There's a whole field over there, so hopefully it's okay to take one. When they bloom, they're all different shades of pink and purple. Wouldn't they look nice out by the fountain?"

"That sounds perfect." He slid an arm around her waist, pulling her close.

She turned her face up to his and planted a quick kiss on his mouth. "And you're feeling all right?"

"Fine." Since they'd moved in together two months ago, he'd had more good days than bad. Some days were harder, with more anxiety, but her support never wavered, and it never would. Some days, he worked from home, and he didn't give himself a hard time about it. Most days, anxiety didn't get the best of him, and he went to work to help other people who might be facing the same thing.

And some other days, days like today, were glorious and perfect. Today, he could have hiked another two miles, out here in the bright sun and wide-open fields.

"Should we head back down the hill?" she asked.

"Before we go, there's one more plant I think you should have."

She glanced over her shoulder at him. "What is it? I probably shouldn't take too many— Oh."

Ben had pulled the ring box out of his pocket, flipped it open, and held it out to her. She stared at it, then her eyes flew to his face. All his prepared words left his head, and he could only stand there and take in her expression of shocked happiness.

Her hand, the one not holding the plant, flew up to cover her mouth. "It's beautiful."

She stared at the ring, but didn't take it out of his hand. The emeralds had been cut and arranged to Ben's exact specifications by the jeweler.

"Is that a ficus leaf?" she asked, reaching her hand out.

"It is a ficus. I knew you'd recognize it. It reminds me of the first time I went out in the van with you."

Her eyes sparkled up at him, gray and bright all at once. "I kidnapped you out of your house."

"You knew what I needed. You've always known." He swallowed. Tried to remember the speech he'd planned for this very important moment. "Nell, I'm sorry. I forgot everything I was supposed to say. I only know I love you. And if you would be my wife, I would be so completely—"

She threw her arms around him, smudging dirt all over his jacket from the uprooted larkspur plant. "Yes. I will. I'll be your wife. I love it. I love you."

"I love you, too. Forever."

She let go of him long enough for him to slide the ring on her finger. He bent his head to kiss the woman he loved.

Chapter 21

There would be many more days, good ones and bad ones. But today was his best day.

A moment later, she held out her hand, studying the ring.

"For a minute there, I wasn't sure if you were going to ask me," she said, her tone teasing.

"If you'd rather wait, I can take it back." Ben reached for her hand, as if to take the ring.

She jerked her arm away. "Oh, no. It's mine now. You'll have to catch me if you want it back."

She turned and took off down the path at a jog. Laughing, Ben ran after her.

Afterword

If you had told ten-years-ago me that I'd be writing books and sharing them with the world, I'd have cried with happiness. It's been a lifelong dream for me, and I've only recently been able to dedicate the time and care needed to bring it to life.

But writing books doesn't happen in a vacuum, and I have so many people I need to thank. Without their help, I wouldn't be doing this.

First, I have to thank my amazing kiddo. When I mentioned several years ago that I'd always wanted to write books, they were the one who told me to try. Without that push, I'm not sure I'd have sat down and actually started to write anything.

To my family, thank you for encouraging me to go on, for being proud of me, and for asking me WHEN you could finally read a draft. I know I'm a self-conscious perfectionist who takes forever to be ready to share anything. But you can read it now!

To my beta readers Rebecca and Jessica, and my sensitivity reader Annie, thank you so much for reading and offering your amazingly helpful feedback.

To my online writing groups, especially the Baguettes and

Romance Schmooze, thank you for the camaraderie, for lifting me up, and for sharing endless valuable information about writing and publishing. It's a big scary world, and you make it easier to navigate.

To the indie publishing community at large, thank you for offering so much advice and information to help new authors like me get started. The wealth of information that's so generously shared is astounding to me.

Thank you, readers, for reading and reviewing indie books. Your review means the world. Thank you for picking up this book and giving it a shot. That's all any author could ever want.

And lastly, thank you to myself, for not giving up on this crazy idea. Ten-years-ago me, we did it. I'm proud of you for keeping on.

About the Author

S.M. Levine grew up with her face in a book, and now she writes steamy, emotional contemporary romance about imperfect people who find true love. She lives in the Midwest with her family and a small assortment of cats.

You can connect with me on:

🌐 https://www.smlevineauthor.com

🔗 https://www.instagram.com/sm_levine

🔗 https://bsky.app/profile/smlevine.bsky.social

Subscribe to my newsletter:

✉ https://www.smlevineauthor.com

Also by S.M. Levine

Check out these other titles in The Well Space series!

The Well Space Series:

Less than Perfect

Trial Run

Couples Session

Over Work (coming fall 2025)